A PAST LESSON

Dedication

To Mum Dad and my brother Robert
for their love and support.

Jennifer Packer

A Past Lesson

REDARROW
BOOKS

A CIP catalogue record for this title is available from the British Library.

ISBN 978 1 84433 011 9

*RedArrow Books is an imprint of
Austin & Macauley Publishers Ltd.*

First Published in 2011

RedArrow Books
CGC-33-01, 25 Canada Square
Canary Wharf, London E14 5LQ

The paper used in this product is grown in sustainable forests

Printed & Bound in Great Britain

2009

Golden sunlight shone down on the dwelling of Emma's childhood home. Autumn leaves littered the long driveway and the impressive building sat as it always had done. Grand in stature but not adorned with unnecessary decoration, its architecture remained unchanged from the simple symmetrical elegance of the late eighteenth century. Emma knew every hue of cream honeyed stone; the daylight seemed to illuminate its proud history, like a man bearing shiny medals on his chest.

She smiled to herself, not once did she think she would see the place again. Whenever her mind did think back, the happiest of memories seemed to be the most painful. Hopes for a future that could never be, nor ever to be, still affected her greatly even after all this time.

She sat on a nearby bench and looked up at one of the sash windows, she remembered sitting at that window looking down on the expensive shiny cars meandering slowly up to the house. Yes she could remember vividly now, they were celebrating, celebrating peace.

The house glowed with soft lighting and beaming faces. Hot rumbling voices filled the busy rooms with news from London. The immaculately dressed servants ran in and out of the house as each guest arrived, placing an umbrella above their heads to protect them from the light mist of rain. Each lady wore expensive pearls, thick furs and long silk dresses. The golden age of peace was to continue, life was to stay carefree. The horrors of the last war would not be repeated. Or so they hoped in 1938.

Autumn 1938

Prime Minister Neville Chamberlain had secured a peace agreement with Adolf Hitler, Great Britain would stay out of all European conflict because diplomatic talks had taken place in Munich and those with a say were happy with the outcome of those talks.

Emma had no thoughts on politics, her main concern that night was looking pretty; she had recently took a liking to one of her brother's friends, they had met at Emma's coming out season and had hoped tonight she might further impress him.

She watched from the upstairs window as the family's black Bentley pulled up. Nickolas was the first out followed by his grandfather. He held out his hand to his mother and grandmother, who quickly disappeared from Emma's view under the umbrella. Nickolas looked up at the window and caught a glimpse of Emma's back as she quickly hurried away from the window.

Jack and William were Emma's elder brothers, a year apart in age, a lifetime apart in maturity. Nickolas excused himself from his grandparents and mother and made his way over to them. "Someone has put on his best eau de cologne," William teased.

"I like to smell my best," Nickolas shrugged.

"Jack don't you agree that Nickolas here is trying to impress someone." He gave a sly smile to his brother.

"I think he is William, looking for a wife. I'm sure." Jack gave Nickolas a pat on the back.

"We will help you get the girl of your dreams, now she is getting on a bit and not much of a looker but by God she can cook!" Doris the cook swung round from her platter of canapés to glare at William, giving him a mock stern face, she then continued with her duties. Nickolas laughed and gave a slight bow to the cook. William soon apprehended her and gave her a small peck on the cheek. "Master Jack you will get me in trouble with your mother, I'm running late as it is." She gave his hand a light slap and waddled off, back to the kitchen.

Emma felt now would be a good time to make her appearance, most people still lingered in the large hall talking, sipping champagne and idling about, not wanting to miss a new face walking through the front door. She carefully glided down the staircase for the full affect, she knew Nickolas would be looking at her, feeling elated, a pretty pink bloom came into her cheeks. "Emma," Nickolas said beaming from ear to ear. "You look beautiful this evening." Catching her eye and making her feel dizzy he asked. "I would like you to meet my grandfather, if that is alright?" Emma followed him with ease and joined her father who was nodding intensely with an elderly gentleman. "Emma this is my grandfather, Alexis Doverenski." He bowed his head at Emma and gave a small smile, then turned back to her father Earl Attwood. "He is not in the best of moods this evening," Nickolas explained.

"Why ever not? Everyone else is, how could he not be in a good mood?"

"I think he and your father are of the same opinion, peace at the expense of others is not peace." He laughed at her confused face, "Come on let's have some champagne."

"I think we have done the right thing, no one wants war. My father fought in the last war, why on earth would he not be celebrating peace?"

"It is not my place to speak for your father, you should ask him. I can only speak for myself and I'm glad to be celebrating the peace agreement, it means I can be with you this evening and can dance without a care in the world." Emma blushed again, excited to be led to the dance floor.

Earl Attwood and the other men sat in the library smoking thick cigars and sipping warming brandy. Each had an idea, a theory on how to curb Hitler's enthusiasm for trampling on other peoples' countries. Harold was unable to keep his thoughts to himself another minute and prompted the soon to be boisterous conversation with one name, Churchill.

"Oh Churchill!" screamed a red faced man. "If he had his way we would all have a spike through our throats by now. A warmonger, thank God for Chamberlain."

"You are all wrong," said one hideously fat chap. "We should be working with Germany, in the last war we were against them and weakened our Empire – better to join them this time and see what spoils we can pick up."

"Despicable, Britain's duty is to protect those small countries against other more powerful forces. That is why we should be in this war now, Churchill is right."

"Attwood live in reality, some are to be rulers, others to be ruled. Our proud history proves which category we are in."

"Do you have no compassion for human life?"

"You're the one who wants to go to war my friend. I think we can safely say life under British rule is more prosperous. We do have superior knowledge on how to run a country."

"I do not feel, we as a nation can make such boasts. Everyone has a right to freedom, to have a say in whom and how their country is run. If British rule were to bring anything to the world I hope a good example of democracy is it."

"Well then you have proven my point; Hitler was voted in, the people of Germany made their choice. So let it be."

"Hitler has abused democracy not championed it!"

"He was voted in fair and square, face it some are a superior race."

"Democracy is also about social equality!"

"Oh now he is a communist! You have spent too much time with your Russian friend over there, comrade Attwood." Alexis reminded the room he had fled from Russia at the start of the Revolution.

"What has taken place in Europe is wrong and we must stop it for the good of mankind. Who knows what Hitler is capable of, action must be taken now. This is only the start, Britain must start building defences. We must realise that going to war is not just about saving our own country but something higher," he paused, "principles. It can and does sometimes mean more than human life."

"I think you should leave politics to those who actually listen to the British people and not to your friend Winston Churchill," scoffed one man, and with that Earl Attwood left the smoke filled room, unable to stomach much more.

As the Evening wound down and guests left, Emma and Nickolas shared a kiss and a promise to take her to the cinema. She wondered how anyone could think of war when such feelings of joy were to be felt.

Emma stood up from the bench and tried to breathe out her apprehension. As the autumn breeze cooled her warm face she continued down the long gravelled path. Her family's home was now a girls' school, a new generation enjoying the walls of Oakwood house. Emma had forgotten how impressive the building was, even with new buildings now surrounding the old manor house, they didn't detract from its beauty, she was happy that time had not changed the exterior. Finally she felt the courage to reach the entrance, walking through the doors she expected to see the old marble flooring and Georgian furniture but was taken aback to find laminate flooring; light painted walls and tall glass wall dividers. Spotlights illuminated the open space; light wooded furniture completed the modern look. The interior was completely different, the staircase was gone from the main hall, the first room Emma had entered was completely unrecognizable to her, and all of a sudden she felt disorientated. Before a wave of sadness could overcome her a woman approached coming through the glass door. "Can I help you?" Despite the kind question, there was no hint of a smile. Emma came to the conclusion she was already an irritation as the elderly always seem to be nowadays. "I said can I help you?" she repeated with exasperation.

"Yes, I'm here to see a Mrs Granger."

"Name?"

"Attwood," she raised herself high. "Lady Emma Attwood." She loved using her full name to obnoxious people.

The receptionist slapped down her papers, turned on her heels and stormed off. Why take a job intending to greet and help people if every request is an annoyance? Emma thought. The tall almost manly looking receptionist came back. "Mrs Granger is on her way. If you would like to take a seat?" She pointed to the chairs with a podgy hand, just as a child feeling unwell came through.

"Miss I feel ill and I have a terrible headache." Her bright red face looked swollen.

"What do you want me to do about it? Go to the sick room." Fat tears welled in the child's eyes as she dragged her school bag behind her.

Emma now knew it had nothing to do with being old, this woman was a cow. "Shouldn't you have asked her what the matter was with her or at least shown some sympathy?" Emma asked.

"She's not dying! It is just an act, probably trying to get out of lessons." Mrs Granger finally arrived.

"I'm so sorry, got held up. How are you Lady Attwood?"

"Well, thank you," Emma replied.

"Mrs Stanley, will you bring us a cup a tea." Turning back to Emma she said, "We will go through to my office."

They walked through the corridors into Mrs Granger's office. "I'm so pleased to have met you Lady Attwood. Has the place brought back many happy memories?"

"Yes many, I would like to thank you for letting me view the old house. You see I have just moved into a new bungalow near to my niece and quite close to the school and I thought I would like to see the old place again."

"Well you are most welcome, I guess inside the place has changed quite a bit."

"At first I thought so but walking past the library I got a faint whiff of my father's cigars."

"Yes it is like mustiness in the walls. Did you have a big family when you lived here?"

"Quite large, I had two brothers and two sisters, all older than me."

"I find all this quite fascinating, I have worked in this school for about eight years, and I became head mistress last year and never knew anything about its history."

"I am happy to tell you all you want to know."

"Perfect I have my notebook ready; I will be showing you around. Oh I hope you don't mind but I have to teach a lesson just before lunch, I thought maybe you could join us and have some input on the girls."

"I'm not one for maths I'm afraid."

Mrs Granger laughed, "No, I'm sorry I had a brainwave this morning and am now getting ahead of myself, I always do when I get excited. I have started teaching my sixth form girls the different situations they might find themselves in. They have all led quite sheltered lives here I think university will be a big culture shock for them."

"I know nothing of the young today."

"I feel that your input into today's discussion will get the girls thinking. Life was so different for you when you were growing up; you grew up in a time when thinking of others was imperative for the nation's survival. It might make them appreciate the opportunities open to them today and I think the girls will respect an older person's point of view." Emma made no reply. "Still I understand if you are too busy and do not want to take part, I'm sorry I should never have asked you."

"Mrs Granger I often read the newspaper and watch the news, I see a rise in binge drinking among young girls. I do not have any comprehension on such behaviour but nor do I feel I have the right to lecture. Every generation has its social problems and I feel I have no advice to give to these young girls."

"Oh but you have, just by living through the decades you have watched how attitudes in women have changed. Today's culture is highly sexed and it is promoted by some as liberation for women and empowerment. I don't want my girls growing up thinking that their bodies are the only way to be successful. I want you to tell them that sexual confidence is one small part of being a woman, they need respect in themselves and I know that is what your generation taught you." Emma smiled at Mrs Granger.

"Not quite, we were done up like turkeys to impress future husbands but to think women are voluntarily going back to that is cause for concern. If you feel I have something to give I will take part."

"I do, this class isn't about the dangers of drink, drugs and alcohol and what it does to the body. They did all that in science; these talks are about the social implications and respecting themselves."

Mrs Granger was someone who Emma thought, viewed the world in black and white. Clearly privately educated herself, she was blessed with more brains than beauty and felt all women should be aiming for academic greatness. Emma placed her age at about mid thirties, her face was small and her neat brunette hair was cut to make a perfect bob. A crisp grey suit finished off with touches of cheap, purple and silver jewellery was a smart, modern, feminine look.

Although Lady Attwood's manner was very friendly and open Jill couldn't help but feel slightly in awe of a superior woman sitting in front of her. Emma held herself with such dignity. It was why she wanted her to talk to the girls; the voice of history was fading everyday, left with dates and timelines and forgetting the ordinary human voice living through extraordinary times. Emma's generation would never have behaved as girls do today, regardless of whether their aims were the same. She felt the bad behaviour of young girls today came from a lack of self-esteem rather than an oafish enjoyment. In her mind Emma's presence could inspire the girls to see themselves with more self-worth.

The tea was brought in. Mrs Stanley's fat bottom eclipsed Mrs Granger's face for a moment as she walked to the side table. "Yes thank you Mrs Stanley." Jill was intrigued by this woman, by her life. Emma had written to her a few weeks ago explaining her link to the school and asked if she may look around the old place, it was her ancestral home. Jill felt she could not refuse but as she read further on she discovered Lady Emma Attwood once worked for the women's land army. She had read about the girls during the war and the hard work they had put in to keep the country fed but somehow she could not marry the two. "Your husband is a peer?"

"No, my father was an Earl. I never married."

"And he was happy for you to be in the land army." Emma's face beamed.

"He threw all his encouragement behind it." Before Jill could ask the question Emma always got asked, she asked Jill first. "Are you married?" Emma knew the answer, she could see her beautiful engagement ring.

"Yes I met Richard here, he was a history teacher and I taught French, but last year I got the job of head mistress and he decided he wanted a change as well. He now deals in antiques selling them on the internet and doing very well."

When the tea was finished, Jill began the tour; Emma roamed around each room with new memories arising fresh in her mind. She felt overjoyed to remember things, she had long forgotten.

As lunch time grew nearer Mrs Granger took Emma into the sixth form common room where her next class would take place. "I think it might be best if the girls call me Miss Attwood. I think they will find it hard enough to connect to me as it is."

"I agree." Jill smiled. She was hopeful with Emma's background and years of experience she would have a really positive affect on the girls and felt she had struck gold with Emma, she seemed modern in many ways and willing to talk about and discuss heavier issues than etiquette and behaviour but also life's difficult situations, in a non-disapproving way.

"The girls you will be meeting are aged between 17 and 18. They are all sixth formers, in their last year here. My discussion group is to help them through their university years, or that's the theory." She held open a large door and continued. "This is the girls' sixth form common room." The large room had sofas and computers lining the walls, windows emitted lots of daylight, it was a perfect room to study. "Some of the girls stay here, some live near by," Jill was explaining. "The sixth formers are allowed out at lunch time but must be back by two. We try to give them responsibility and a little independence." A bell rang and the young girls started to make their way into the common room. "Miss Attwood if you could sit over there?"

Emma sat down and watched how the girls threw themselves into the sofas. "Girls settle down please, we have a visitor taking part in today's lesson. Miss Attwood grew up here and worked for the women's land army during the Second World War. She has seen how women's attitudes have changed from work to love to family. Today's women have a lot more choices and independence and I would like you all to think seriously on where you would like your lives to go. Tell me girls where do you see yourselves in ten years time?"

Some said actresses, a few said models, or a good career but most said married with children. It struck Emma that time may separate them but their hopes and dreams had not changed all that much.

"Was that how it was for you Miss Attwood?" Mrs Granger asked.

"Our main concern was getting married and finding the right man. Of course when war broke out women had to work to keep the country going. I think it was then that the world for women started to change – work does bring a sense of freedom. It is nice to do something you feel passionate about, but after the war us girls were expected to go back to being housewives and many resented this. It was the start of the female revolution; we wanted to be free to make our own choices and not to rely on a father or husband to do it."

One girl asked if raising a family is enough in today's world, "Has the female revolution put too much pressure on women? Now aren't you expected to do it all?"

"Not at all," said Mrs Granger. "It is your choice what you want to do and mustn't feel pressured by the outside world."

"But what are we meant to be doing working or raising a family?" another girl asked. "It seems to me it is previous generations who has heaped so much pressure on women. No wonder why we are so confused. You came before us and you tell us how to look, how we must achieve a great career and raise the perfect family. Then you complain at young girls who cannot achieve getting a boyfriend let alone a job and we feel like the failure. It is your generation who has piled on the pressure of the perfect way of life, which is completely unachievable and then you wonder why we get drunk and have no self-esteem. And why we look to men for vindication because they are an easy way to feel good about ourselves."

"That is exactly what I am saying; we must all accept the hardships of life with dignity. Alright so you might not be the sharpest tool in the box but that does not mean you should degrade yourself. I feel you all have something to offer and whether that is being a doctor or being a mother, it is an important contribution to life."

Mrs Granger finished her sentence and looked over to a blonde girl who seemed bored in the corner of the room. "Have you got anything to contribute Matilda?"

Her gaze turned from her teacher to Emma. "Why are you a Miss and not a Mrs? Were you never married?" she asked with little subtlety.

"Matilda!" shouted Mrs Granger. "You certainly need to learn some manners! That was very rude."

"It's alright," Emma said, she had nothing to hide. She turned back to the blonde haired girl slumped in the sofa. She took a long look at her before answering. "No, marriage did not happen for me, dear."

"Oh, Miss Attwood," Mrs Granger exclaimed, "you can't call the pupils 'dear'. It's not politically correct."

"In that case," said Emma thinking fast and turning back to Matilda, "I will forgive you for asking me an impertinent question, if you forgive my clearly offensive name calling."

Mrs Granger's eyes widened in complete shock. Matilda's smile was stretched over her face, she thought that was exactly the type of sarcastic comment she would make. Jill managed to pull herself together with a loud clearing of her throat. "As you can see Miss Attwood, girls today are blunt."

"Honestly it is fine. If people tiptoed around we would never get anywhere. No I never did marry."

"So you won't be giving us a sex education?" All the girls fell about giggling but the shock tactic failed on Emma.

"That is enough Matilda I am trying to have an important adult conversation with you all." Matilda merely smirked.

"I think we all know the facts of life Miss. We don't need you talking to us about men. We know how to pull 'em. We don't need you telling us how we need to be treated by them."

"By your sheer immature behaviour, I think you do."

Emma spoke up, she wanted to avoid saying 'when I was young' because things were so different then but felt it needed to be said for them to know that she didn't expect them to walk about in a hat and gloves and borrowing their grandmothers twin set and pearls. "When I was young, we never had any lessons such as this. We were taught how to walk and talk; we were not expected to do anything other than to marry. I know with magazine and television you girls are not as naive as we were and so never knew the risks involved of let's say getting drunk. Such things were not tolerated but that doesn't mean to say it didn't go on because it did and if those young girls did find themselves in trouble they were completely alone. I'm sure you think you know everything but you don't. Your teacher is trying to make you stop and think about the dangerous situations you might have to face. You say the generations before you makes you feel inferior but if it wasn't for them you would not have their knowledge of how to deal with a difficult situation because it only comes with age and experience, which is why your teacher is talking to you. You are luckier than you realise which is why you should not cheapen yourselves."

Matilda, who had long blonde hair, bright blue eyes and an aura of self-confidence but one that Emma felt was put on, once again fell silent.

"Exactly, I want you girls to see that nothing is stopping you from achieving whatever you want to achieve. It is not like Miss Attwood's day when they had a war to fight and life became an uncertainty. You have everything before you and I want you to make the most of it." Matilda looked up once again.

"This class is pointless, it is no longer, 1940 or whatever era you come from." She glared at Emma. "I know how to handle myself and I do not need you patronizing me." Defiance ran through her eyes, like a bull ready to charge.

"I think you should leave Matilda, I do not know what has got into you but I have heard quite enough."

"You are deluded if you think bringing a batty old woman is going to inspire us to be frigid. We are all going off to university next year, to sleep around and get completely drunk. We won't care what other people think of us so long as the barman serves us drinks, we won't even know anyone else is there."

"Everything I deplore in young women you have just said." Matilda fell quiet again, she tried hard to control her anger but it kept getting the better of her. "When you are under the influence of alcohol, you're not in control of yourself. You are vulnerable and people – men – can take advantage. You could get so inebriated, that you instigate a whole night of passion and not remember it the next morning."

Matilda flared up. "So we have to live like nuns."

"I want you leave, go and stand outside my office I will speak to you later." Mrs Granger had had enough of this petulant girl.

Matilda left with a slam of the big door, Mrs Granger had done so much for her but she could not suppress those feeling of hate and jealously.

"I think you should all do a project on the dangers of alcohol abuse," Mrs Granger said after Matilda had gone. The bell rung signalling end of lesson and Emma gave Mrs Granger a sympathetic smile. "Sorry that could have gone so much better. I really thought I could help them see their potential."

"They are still children in many ways."

"No, that is what is so worrying, they are adults and we are just not teaching them how to be good ones. Matilda was always going to be difficult. I used to be her form teacher before I took the new job as head mistress. My relationship with her has always been good, she hasn't had it easy and maybe I have been too nice to her. Over these past few weeks she has been acting very strangely."

"Maybe I could talk to her?"

"Thank you but no you see she has had it tough and I don't think she would want to speak to a stranger about her problems."

"I understand."

"I hope you have enjoyed looking round."

"Yes it has evoked a lot of memories and reminded me of the choices I made when I was young. It's amazing after all these years nothing much has changed. Goodbye Mrs Granger it was a pleasure to meet you."

Emma's niece drove up in her black mini to the school entrance to meet Emma. "How was it?" she asked as Emma got in.

"I met her; I knew her instantly, she looked just like my mother. It gave me quite a shock."

"You met her? Will you tell her who you are?"

"I can't just blurt out to someone I have just met, I fell in love and had an affair with a married man during the war and as a result you are my granddaughter."

"But you will never see her again if you don't."

"I will just have to be grateful I got to see her today."

"What do you want to do now?"

"I want to have a nice cup of tea."

Winter 1938

Harold slammed down his newspaper with some velocity, everyone looked up but no one uttered a word. Emma adored her father and knew him to be a man of fairness and good humour, this brooding quiet and quick temped man was one she had never witnessed. She wasn't frightened of him, his character had not changed, but she just knew something was very wrong in the world for her father to be so distant from them all. With another sigh, (it had become a habit) Harold spoke to his family. "What is everyone doing today?"

His two eldest daughters made their excuses with their husbands and left, everyone could sense Harold's mood and no one wanted to be left to his angry political ramblings.

Next his two sons grabbed the final pieces of toast and said they were walking to the village 'to get some air', this was code to one another but everyone knew it meant chat up girls. It just left his wife Clarice and Emma, "Father why are you so upset with peace, I don't understand you have always said war is abhorrent. Why are you so angry that we have been saved from the horrors of it?"

Clarice glared at her daughter, "I have some flowers to arrange." And with that she breezed out of the breakfast room.

"It is not that I don't want peace, of course I do but at this moment in time it is simply not possible. How can we live in peace knowing the rest of Europe is going to suffer all over again? Czechoslovakia has been broken up without them having any sort of say in it and this coming from so called democratic countries. The injustice is sickening."

"But I thought Hitler got the German speaking parts, isn't that fair?"

"No they have ripped apart a country and destroyed peoples' lives and given them no voice to fight for what belongs to them, no that is not fair. Britain has always been a beacon of honour and justice, Chamberlain has swept it all aside, how will we look in history?"

"I suppose this little episode will be forgotten in time as people rebuild their lives."

"Emma we are not dealing with rational people, today Czechoslovakia, tomorrow someone else. We cannot believe a word he says, we must start preparing ourselves otherwise it will be too late. Hitler will get more and more powerful, the more we give into him the less chance we have to standing up to him."

"Father you're frightening me."

"I'm sorry Emma but life looks very uncertain, if the worse should happen we will go to America. But do not believe the newspapers or the government, dark clouds are forming and they will rain upon us, if Chamberlain does not put up his umbrella."

2009

Emma started her usual morning ritual of buying the day's newspapers and making her way into a small coffee shop. Her breakfast every morning was the same, two toasted crumpets, one with cheese, one with honey and a mug of milky coffee. There she would sit quite happily until mid morning, often having a chat with the waitress who had now memorized her order. She enjoyed the peace of her long morning, it helped her mull over anything which had taken place the pervious day.

It had been a week since she had gone back to her old home and a week since she dreamt of him. Up until that point her images of him had been vague, but arriving back had evoked the most vivid of memories. Even the young Nickolas came fresh into her mind, happy, happy times spent with him. She was in this dreamy state when someone sat in front of her without a word of warning. "I saw you from over the road." She pointed out the window to where she was standing. "I thought I better come over."

"It's Matilda isn't it?" Emma asked feeling slightly dazed.

"Yep, look I wanted to say sorry for being so rude, I should never have got so angry."

"Apology accepted. Although I do not think it is me that you need to say sorry to. Mrs Granger cares very deeply for you all; she wants you to achieve your very best and to be happy."

"I know, I know but she is so out of touch. I learnt all this rubbish years ago. I watch Sex and the City. I know how to look after myself. I know the difference between love and lust."

"I admit you do know a lot about life, far more than I probably know today with all of my life experience but don't shut yourself off to those people who want to help you."

"Why did Mrs Granger ask you to speak to us? Not being funny but you're hardly likely to understand what we are going through."

"I suppose it is different perspective on life she wanted you to see. We were brought up so differently."

"Things move on." She shrugged. "Why didn't you ever marry?" Matilda asked out of the blue. "Didn't you ever fall in love?"

26

"I did fall in love and more than once but when the time came, I don't know, I feared something and could never make that final commitment. I was asked, time and time again but I could never open up to him, not fully anyway. I thought if I can't be honest with the man I plan to marry then clearly I should not be marrying him."

"Didn't you ever have that one love that made you feel all fuzzy inside?"

"You're talking about first love, yes I had that. His name was Nickolas."

"What happened?"

Emma thought back to her first heart flutters over Nickolas but the spell was broken when the waitress reappeared. "More coffee?"

"Two more please." The waitress walked back to the coffee bar. "War broke out and we separated. What about you? Have you ever been in love?"

"Tell me about Nickolas!" Matilda did not want to confide but she hoped Emma would.

Spring 1939

Emma's mother Lady Clarice Attwood had tried several times to extract information from Jack about a lad called Nickolas Doverenski, who Emma had been stepping out with. Jack and Nickolas had been at school with each other and had introduced him to his sister at a party. Despite his mother's clever questioning, Jack managed to give an answer without actually answering anything. "Doverenski, is that a popular Russian name?" Clarice tried to subtly persuade her son into telling her whether Nickolas came from a wealth family.

"I think it is well known in Russia." Jack shrugged.

"You mean it's a common surname?"

"No." His eyes were glinting with humour.

"Stop this Jack and tell me all you know about him. I can't remember seeing his father at the Party? What does he do?"

"Nothing he's dead."

"Dead! Oh dear. Is there a high death toll in his family?"

"No. Just him."

"What did he die of?"

"I think…" he said, as he started to walk away. "The same thing as the cat."

"O dear God! What was it?"

"Curiosity."

"Jack come back here at once! This is your sister we are talking about and I am concerned for her." Jack turned back to his mother and gave a long sigh, he hated giving in to her melodramas.

"I have heard rumours about his mother." Clarice lowered her voice. "I heard she has never been married so how do you explain her son?"

"I don't think you have to be married to reproduce…"

"Enough, you know what I mean she a loose character, so I have been told, takes his grandfather's name does he not?"

"His father *so I have been told* returned to Russia a few years back, he fell ill and died. His grandfather wanted him to take his surname as he does not have a son to carry on the name as well as the businesses. His grandfather is quite wealthy as far as I know."

"Well, what does his grandfather do?"

"Do you know I never thought to ask!" he replied mockingly.

"I don't believe all that guff about his father dying, all sounds very odd to me and the way I saw his mother knocking back the champagne. I don't think she is a woman of virtue."

"Mother please don't be rude to him, he is rather a good chap. Life hasn't been exactly easy on any of them, so please have a little compassion."

"I am always compassionate! I wanted to know he if was good enough for my daughter, it is a mother's right."

"Well take it from me; he is a good chap with a kind heart, who I think is falling deeply in love with Emma."

Clarice softened, "If that is true, then I'm happy."

Emma couldn't stand her mother's judgemental eye on Nickolas whenever he came to the door. A hundred questions would be fired at him and never given enough time to answer. So they came up with an idea to avoid her.

Outside her bedroom window Nickolas stood throwing small pebbles at it. "Good afternoon." He tried to speak in a loud whisper. Emma smiled down nervously; she was trying to climb out of her window for the first time. A wisteria tree clung to the wall, its heady scent made her feel dizzy, huge purple flowers clouded her view down, bees buzzed around her and worst of all she wasn't quite sure if the plant could take her weight. After a few nervous minutes she stepped down and so they set off to walk the grounds, hand in hand. They stopped at Emma's favourite place; it always reminded her of a Gainsbourgh's painting of the newly married couple Mr and Mrs Andrews. The landscape was similar, with a huge oak tree but next to her oak tree ran a soft stream. Beneath the tree they sat, arms round each other. Blissfully unaware of anything that could destroy their uneventful future together.

"I was so contented; he was a lovely looking boy. Dark chocolate brown eyes, dark hair." Emma's mind was starting to daydream.

"Love at first sight," Matilda said.

"Yes, I had the hots for him as you say nowadays." Emma giggled. Matilda rolled her eyes but let her continue, "I think I loved him right from the start but there is a huge difference from being in love and loving someone."

"How so?"

"If you are in love with someone, you love the idea of them. If you love someone you see their faults but love that person in spite of them." This to Matilda was wrong how anyone could love someone who isn't perfect. "I need passion and excitement in my life," she declared.

"But it will always end in heartbreak," Emma said.

"Better that than never knowing it." The hot coffees were brought to the table, "I would like a piece of cake as well please," Matilda ordered, she was enjoying her chat with Miss Attwood and wanted to prolong it.

She started to question Emma again. "So what happened between you and Nickolas?"

"We had a fling, I guess that is what you would call it nowadays and when war came we went our separate ways."

This completely puzzled Matilda. "Weren't you two going out with each other?"

"What does that mean? Anyway we were sweethearts but he broke it off with me before he left for the war, I don't know why but I remember feeling so devastated. He told me he did not believe people could fall in love with the first person they met or he didn't want to believe it. Like you I dreamed of someone who was utterly devoted to me and I thought that was him."

"Why did he break it off, you both seemed so in love?"

"I suppose the thought of war does funny things, many people got married, I got dumped."

"How old was he when he went to war?"

"Nineteen, seems so young now but it was war and we just got on with it."

"There wasn't much of an age gap then."

"What a strange thing to say. And anyway there was enough to make me feel excited."

"Did you love him though, deep down?" Matilda asked earnestly.

"I loved being with him, I suppose having a boyfriend is having a walking statement, 'someone finds me attractive'. I was sensible though, we never crossed those boundaries."

"You mean you didn't have sex." Matilda put it bluntly.

"No, unlike today it was a great scandal if a girl got pregnant without being married. Girls would risk their lives to avoid society discovering she was with child. I could not take that risk, what with my family being so..." Emma trailed off; remembering Matilda had no idea who she was.

"At least those girls didn't mean to get up the duff! Unlike nowadays every girl seems to be popping one out."

"Mistakes happen, we shouldn't be too judgemental," Emma warned her.

"Maybe, it's certainly not the life I would choose."

"Good for you. Plenty time for all of that."

"Did you have children?" This startled Emma.

"No. Anyway I've told you about my life, time to tell me about yours. Do you have a boyfriend?"

"There is someone." She smiled slyly but suddenly dropped her head.

"Who is it?"

"You wouldn't understand, you've probably never done anything wrong."

"Of course I have." She took a slow slurp of the now cooled coffee. "I can tell something is upsetting you. I want you to know anything you tell me, I will keep to myself."

Matilda quickly pulled herself together, "There is nothing wrong, it's just exam stress that sort of thing. I'm going to go and look in that clothes shop, want to come with me?"

"Alright but you must be back by two."

"Anything you want to look at?"

"No, I just want to make sure you get back to school on time, you don't want to lose your privileges."

Emma sat down in the shoe section of the shop and watched the different girls looking at different clothes. She could over hear one girl saying to another, "I've got a date tonight, hope I get lucky."

"Is that with Sean the mail guy?"

"Yeah! Well fit!" This girl was quite podgy, the material revealed her weight in the most unflattering way making her look ten times bigger and a hundred times cheaper. "Perfect," she said to her friend.

"Slapper," Matilda whispered.

"Have you got what you want?" Emma asked her.

"Yes thanks and ready to go when you are."

"What did you buy?"

"Just some underwear."

As Emma got up to leave, the podgy girl reappeared in her work clothes, the shirt was too tight, the buttons strained and she could see a pink bra through the gaps. It really completed the look of vulgar.

"Please don't say you bought a pink bra?" Emma begged as they made their way to the bus stop.

"No," she laughed knowing exactly why Miss Attwood was appalled. "Well I guess this is goodbye."

"I will walk back with you, I live down Maynard road near to the school."

"I know where that is, it's not that far but let's take the bus I feel quite lazy."

When they had arrived back to the school, Matilda thanked Miss Attwood for her company, it was good to speak to someone completely different and Miss Attwood had been really nice and understanding. "What is your next lesson?" Emma inquired.

"I have English, ah and it starts in five minutes, bye Miss Attwood." She started to walk away but not towards the main entrance, Emma was annoyed that Matilda could show such contempt for her after all she had done. She waited a few moments, and then slowly followed in the same direction. Matilda had led her to a cottage, the driveway was hidden by large plants and the house sat right back from view. Emma knew the cottage very well, but could not work out why Matilda would go there. She sat on her bench and came to the decision that as she had not seen Matilda enter the cottage, she did not want to make assumptions. After a little rest, Miss Attwood made her way back to the bus stop and back home; she thought maybe it wasn't such a good idea investigating too closely. No good could come of it.

Nickolas watched Emma run about with her sisters and brothers. Her face alight with happy joy and thrill. His feeling for her had intensified more than he thought possible, her sweetness had enlightened his soul and he knew in his heart she was the one he wanted to marry.

Emma had enjoyed every minute she had spent with Nickolas and believed herself to be head over heels in love with him. She was sure an engagement would come soon and excited to hear him speak of the future and plans he was making.

"Your father asked to see my grandfather today, I think they have guessed my feelings for you."

"What are your feelings?" she teased

"I love you, Emma. I love every second of your company and want to have your company forever." Emma's colour rose is delight.

"Why does your grandfather call you Nickoli?"

"I was named after the Russian Tsar Nickolas the second. He likes to remind himself of Russia."

"Family is very important to my mother; I hope nothing stands in the way of us."

Lord Attwood knew of Emma's growing attachment to Nickolas and he thought a lot of the boy but Clarice had expressed some concern of the family. He knew it was time to question Nickolas's grandfather and his friend Alexis. Alexis' past had been a blur he felt he had no choice but to ask him directly how he had made his way to England.

Alexis' story begins in Russia, born to a well-connected aristocratic family, the revolution of 1917 had their houses and belongings stripped and ripped apart, all they could take were themselves and a few bits of jewellery that Natalya his wife hid on her person and their daughter who was fourteen at the time. An English journalist helped them escape with fake identification papers, they took a train out of Moscow to Petrograd, even their clothes had to be rags so as not to raise suspicion, from Petrograd on to Finland, where fake papers had to be shown, from there onto a boat to reach Sweden, Denmark from there a long boat trip to

England. Many went to France but this journalist promised to help them and he did not let them down. He found them a room to rent and paid for the first few weeks and although most were hostile to Alexis, a job was found. He carried heavy stock for a small corner shop. The old man who ran the shop was fast running out of energy, he had to carry on working though, his wife and their two daughters and three grandchildren depended on him. Their husband had not returned from the Great War and he had no one to help him with the business. Alexis took over and managed the shop and then expanded the business. In five years they had amassed eight small stores dotted all around London. Sadly the old man died Alexis kept one shop back for his widow and family, the rest he sold and divided the profits. It was then he purchased his first factory and started to produce cigarettes.

Lord Attwood was of course impressed with Alexis' self-prevention. "That damn war, we are no better off now than we were then," Lord Attwood said.

"It's ironic the Royal families, who say they are chosen by God, argue and get everyone else involved in their bickering. So we say no, we can choose better, we are better judges of character, turns out we are not."

"We are most defiantly heading back for war, Germany is now after Poland. Chamberlain has put a guarantee on it but it will not stop Hitler. Whether we will stand by our guarantee is another question? But sooner or later we will have to fight."

"For Great Britain's sake I hope it is sooner, Hitler is becoming more powerful and he has got powerful friends. There are some rumours Stalin and Hitler have opened up talks, if you do not make Russia an ally we are in desperate times."

"If that is true, we are done for. War looks as if it is imperative, get your grandson married to my girl. Who knows how long they will have together?"

Matilda ran out of her French class with Mrs Granger and left for lunch, she knew if she hurried she would catch Miss Attwood leaving the café with her big pile of newspapers in her big shopper. She had decided she liked Miss Attwood, she was uncomplicated and she listened plus she was interested in Emma's past life, a part of her was curious about her time growing up and she satisfied herself with the thought Emma wanted to talk about it, all old people do.

"Hey I thought I'd find you here!" she panted with breathlessness.

"Here I am, you wanted to see me?" Emma asked bemused.

"You were telling me about Nickolas your first love, well I want to hear more."

"I will tell you more in time but first tell me about you. Have things improved between you and Mrs Granger?"

"Oh, Mrs Granger is always interfering and patronizing me. I think she actually picks on me on purpose."

"Why would you think that?"

"I don't know. I just do."

"Tell me about yourself then, your family and friends."

"What's to tell?" she shrugged. "I was always meant to go to this school but my mother walked out on me when I was ten, she had some sort of break down, it was when my grandmother died, they were very close. My father couldn't cope and I was sent to my aunt's to live in Cornwall, I think he did it to punish me. Anyway after a while my aunt got sick of me and father decided to send me here. Mrs Granger was my form teacher and she made sure I was happy here." Matilda lowered her head, almost in shame.

"Do you remember anything about your mother?"

"Yes, lots of things. The way she laughed, the way she smelt, lots of things. I guess she never loved me, the truth is no one ever has."

Emma's heart broke in two, tears started to form in her eyes, she bit her lower lip and blinked hard. "Don't push away those people who want to help you. Mrs Granger cares for you and I'm sure your father loves you very much, he must have gone through a terrible time himself." Matilda dried her cheeks with a thin paper napkin.

"I've done something awful, I don't deserve to be loved or cared for."

"Of course you do, whatever you have done it can be fixed."

"I better get back, sorry to burden you, I won't let it happen again."

"Don't go. You wanted to hear more about Nickolas and me? I will tell you."

"Ok. I'll just go to the bathroom and freshen myself up. Could you order me some food and a coffee, here is ten pounds." She handed the note to Emma, for Emma to hand it back.

"No, that's alright, my treat and listen you can come and talk to me anytime and I am sure Mrs Granger is the same, you do have people around you who care."

"Thank you." Emma's words were meant to bring comfort but she could see Matilda's pain etched across her face. Something had gone very wrong in Matilda's life and the one person she had become close to now seemed worlds apart. Emma knew she would have to speak to Jill but wondered if that would be betraying Matilda's confidence.

Autumn 1939

Rain drizzled down beneath Nickolas's coat, it seeped into his skin, yet he could not feel this coldness for the coldness he felt inside was much icier. All of his dreams for the future had been snatched and bitterness overwhelmed him. He ran round to Emma's window hoping she was sitting in her room reading; the way he was feeling he did not want to see Clarice.

His anger was burning, Emma was the only one he wanted to be with and it was all about to be taken away.

She heard the light taps from the small pebbles on her window, as she expected Nickolas was standing underneath soaked to the skin.

"What are you doing, go to the front door I will let you in."

"I need to speak to you alone." He started to climb the wisteria before Emma could dissuade him.

"What's wrong?"

"Have you not heard? Hitler and Stalin have made a non-aggression pact."

"Yes but how does that affect us?"

"It means Britain has lost a potential ally and has thrown suspicion on all Russians."

"This doesn't change my feeling for you."

"My grandfather has said we will just lie low and see it through but my mother is being difficult. She has met some American guy and is marrying him next week. Mother wants me to stay with her and take this guy's surname to hide my Russian blood. My grandfather went ballistic. You think she would be a bit more grateful to him or at least show some respect for his feelings. I love my mother but I can't stand the way she treats grandfather Alexis."

"Is it really that bad?"

"If they are not talking then they are arguing. Mother has met this new man and wants to move to America. Fine said grandfather but don't think you are taking Nickoli." Nickolas did his best Russian accent. "Then she went on how I was her son and I will go where she wants me to go."

"But we are engaged?" Emma's heart raced with fear, she couldn't bear the thought of not being with Nickolas.

"No one thought to ask me what I wanted and no I would not go anywhere without you."

"You should take off that coat off; I will get you a towel to dry yourself."

"Emma." She stopped to turn back to him. "I can't marry you, you know I want to but I have no money, I need to get a job but grandfather won't let me, he wants me to work in the family business, under the family name. I tried to tell him no one will want to buy Doverenski cigarettes and no one else will give me a job with such a name, I have nothing to offer you."

"Things have a way of working themselves out. Your grandfather is right, people will soon move on. She can't make you go to America."

"Yes she can, you see when my grandfather was working every hour God gave him she started to enjoy the night clubs, jazz bars and such. She got pregnant one night with me. She has no idea who my father was and very little shame in admitting that. To my grandfather's credit he stood by her, raised me and has cared for me ever since. She argues he has too much control over me and threatens him, that she would tell the world that my father did not die when he went back to Russia but that I am a bastard and no one will want to do business with such a disreputable family."

"My mother must never know about this."

"That is what I am saying, I cannot marry you, either way our engagement could not be made public. I don't know what will happen and sooner or later you will get bored of waiting."

"Never, I love you Nickoli Doverenski. We will wait until something sorts itself out."

Harold had come to London to help his son-in-laws' move their small law firm to the country. The whole of London was preparing and no one held out any hope that war would not take place. After having read the day's news he burst his way into his men's club, he had jumped over many sandbags and dodged men carrying shelter apparatus while waving the newspaper high in the air, "Chamberlain is making a war cabinet and guess who is once again Lord High Admiral, yes yes Winston! Finally someone who talks sense and can take this lot on."

Back at the country estate, everyone was called into Earl Attwood's office, all the family and staff gathered in the large room. The family seating themselves on dark brown leather sofas while the staff made a semicircle around the room. Harold stood by his desk with a large tumbler of whisky sitting near his right hand and in his left a fat cigar swirled smoke into the air. "As you all know war has been announced. I doubt it came as much of a surprise but it will affect us all and I want us all to contribute to the war effort." Everyone nodded in agreement.

"This is a good time to tell you all then," William started to say but Jack decided to intervene hoping that his mother would deal with the news easier if he could put it to her gently, unlike William who was ready to blurt it out. "Mother, Father. William and I have decided to join the RAF."

"There is no need for all that!" Clarice shouted.

"Mother, it is an opportunity for us."

"You are twenty-one, William you're just twenty. You are too young to die in a heap of metal and for a war that will last only a few months!"

"But think of the women! They won't be able to keep their hands off of us," William said as he winked at a maid, who blushed crimson and put her eyes to the floor.

"You may go now." Clarice ordered the servants away. Jack looked imploringly at his father.

"Clarice, the boys want to do this, just like I wanted to do my bit when I was young. You may be right and this war might last only a few months but whatever happens at least our boys will know they did their duty." He felt sick as he said it, other boys would have to fight through and his were no different.

Clarice walked out of the room unable to stifle her tears; her daughters followed her out, trying in vain to console her.

"You do understand father? We have to do our bit." Jack was concerned his father might force him to stay to make sure he would inherit.

"Of course, I am proud of you both."

"We are going in together, we will come out together'" William declared.

"We need a strong drink, whisky lads?"

"No thanks, we are going down to the 'Barn', tell all the girls

40

of our up and coming adventures." William gave his father a cheeky smile and left with Jack following behind.

Finally Harold turned to his sons'-in-law, "What about you two, Henry, Derek, Whisky?" They both nodded their replies and Harold poured two doubles.

"What do you make of this war, sir?" asked Henry.

"Chamberlain thinks Hitler will be assassinated at some point or Germany will be staved into submission."

"You do not think that is true?"

"None of us do. The man is delusional, if we stood up and listened to the French from the outset, we would be in a much better position. I do not hold up much chance of us winning this war, not unless America joins and why would they? We have left it too late, Winston told them all. Hitler will not stop his world domination, we have given him an inch in the past and he took a mile. Now he is too powerful and has very powerful friends. No I do not hold up much hope." Both the men nodded glumly, "What will you two do?" Harold asked the question both were now contemplating.

"I guess wait until we are called up," Derek said.

"You will fight then?"

Henry put his head in his hands, Maria was pregnant with their first child, how could he leave for war? However, he could not walk away when his country needed him. "Yes, as you say we need to do our duty."

"What about the company?" Henry and Derek met at university, both were studying law, after they had achieved their degrees, they decided to go into partnership and set up their own small law firm. Thanks to their fathers' investments, the small law firm was now doing very well.

"We will just have to close it down until we get back."

Fear hung in the air, Harold gulped down the last dregs of whisky. "What a difference a year makes."

2009

Emma had rung Jill earlier in the week to make an appointment with her. Matilda's tearful confession had played on Emma's mind for days, she knew that it was not her place to get involved but she would never forgive herself if she turned a blind eye to someone suffering. "Lady Attwood how nice to see you again, how have you been?"

"Very well, thank you. I know you are busy so I will get straight to the point. A few days ago Matilda met me in a café, we got talking and she confided in me of her difficult past. She is feeling very rejected and I think she has done something silly. I don't know what, she did not say but I know she wants to talk about this to someone and I think she needs you."

"She has been acting very strangely, I spoke to her on that day she had that tantrum. It was very out of character for her but she said sorry and didn't want to discuss it any further."

"I am most concerned for her. Has her father been in contact?"

"He writes to her every two weeks or so but I have heard nothing from him nor has she confided to me what is in those letters. Lady Attwood I think Matilda sees something in you, I see it too, and it is kindness. Obviously she feels happy to talk to you, as long as you don't mind; if she is bothering you then I will talk to her."

"She is not bothering me, like I said I am just concerned for her, she seems very alone."

"I will keep an eye. Sorry to change the subject but I am glad you phoned. I was writing a new booklet on the school, we like to give them out at open days and then I had a brain wave, I could do a small section on the history of the building. I think it would really interest some of the parents and even some of the pupils."

"I would love to take part in that, my father would have been so happy. He was devastated when the place was sold. Jack was seriously injured in the war and could not cope with the house and as for William, well flighty is too loose of a description. It was going to go to Bernadette and her husband Derek but he wanted a new life away from it all. The entire landscape looked like the battlefield. We had all sorts of things going on to help the war effort. My father continued running the place until the late sixties, I think he hoped Derek would change his mind but he had a new life and he did not want to come back. The war was tough on many and he did not need."

Winter 1939

Emma sat on the windowsill and looked out over the vast amount of land, covered in a thick mass of snow. Strange how everything seemed still, like it was so cold everything had frozen and the world was unmoved. Behind her the door opened quickly making her jump, for a moment Nickolas stood in front of her before sitting down next to her on the windowsill. Emma started to talk, "Despite the snow, I don't feel the magic of winter or of Christmas. Normally everything looks so beautiful, now the cold just feels depressing."

"It's too cold that's why."

"Maybe."

"Emma," Nickolas was now staring at her awkwardly. "You know we had these plans for us to marry and live happily ever after?"

"Had? You must mean have."

"No."

"I don't understand, your mother is not getting married she is staying here. Your grandfather has forgiven her. We have nothing standing in our way."

"I feel I must join up to the army, I will be called up at some point but I would like to volunteer. As Russia will not be joining the war, Britain will need all the men it can get and I was born in this country and I will fight for this country."

"We are engaged, you promised you loved me. You promised. You promised to always love me."

"Emma I do not have time for your childish tears. Love can last a night, it can last day or it can last a lifetime but it does not last forever."

"You do not love me anymore?" He looked into her wide, red eyes filled with heartache and felt his own soul being torn. He had tried to break away from her before now he must be more forceful, even though it broke his heart.

"As you know things have been tense at home for me. This gives me a good excuse to get out."

"I will wait until you get back. Nickolas I love you. I dream about our future together everyday. I see you looking at me from down the aisle, holding our first child, laughing when we are old. You see those things too?"

"I feel it is wrong of me to ask you to wait for me."

"I will though, I said I will forever."

"No, my feelings for you have changed," he lied, "and I doubt I will be coming back. You must move on with your life and forget me."

"Nickolas, this isn't you. Please don't treat me so cruelly." She held tight to his waist, crying upon his shoulder. He wanted to comfort her to tell her that he still loved her and his heart was in as many pieces as hers but there was no getting away from war. He knew getting over hatred was a lot easier than grief. He did not want her to feel bound to him if the worst should happen, life must continue for her.

"It is time I left."

"Please don't say that."

He wrapped his arms around her waist, giving in to his own need of comfort. "It's for the best, we will always be friends."

"Nickolas, I…" He stopped her by kissing her lips, before she would say something he could not bear to hear again. Then reluctantly he let her go, he longed to stay, to tell her how he really felt but could not put her through it and so they parted.

Emma watched the snow falling; it seemed to fall in perfect unison with her tears. She watched Nickolas walk away from the house and felt overwhelmed to run to him. With Nickolas going off to war her emotions were heightened, she wished she could wail and scream until he changed his mind. However much she willed herself to call to him, she could not do it and she hated herself for it. It was a bizarre feeling, desperation mixed with overwhelming hurt. She wondered if she would ever see him again and with that thought every tear that once sat dormant in her eyes now flowed free. It would takes weeks before Emma emerged from her room and by then Nickolas had signed up and left.

The skies were growing darker, winter was becoming bitingly cold, and Emma knew it was an omen. The world was freezing, becoming heartless, just like people and their lives. All dreams of the future died, as who knew if anyone of them had a future.

Mr and Mrs Granger's cottage was the one Emma thought she saw Matilda go into but it seemed doubtful, that was until she met Mr Richard Granger, tall, dark and handsome. Straight away they looked like an odd couple, Richard's movie star looks, completely eclipsed Jill's plain but not unattractive appearance. "How long have you two been married?"

"Six years, I could not believe it when he asked me!" Jill exclaimed. "We were both working together."

"I used to be a teacher as well," Richard clarified.

"He used to be a history teacher," Jill interrupted.

"Jill got the top job at Oakwood last year and then thought it would be good for me to do something different so I set up my own antiques business."

"Very impressive, do you ever think about teaching again?"

"No not at all. I am thinking about writing a book and Jill was explaining how she wanted a little bit written about this place."

"A very good place to start, well I am happy to help."

"It is quite amazing just one family lived there, it is so big."

"It does seem a lot bigger than it was, but yes this place belonged to my father, he sold when no one wanted to take it over."

"How old is it?"

"Late Georgian I would say, dates around the late 1700s to the start of the 1800s."

"Wow, had it been in your family all that time?"

"Yes, someone must have been friendly with old Prinny George IV. It was always a mystery, at that time most people were losing money at the gaming table."

Jill sat down next to Richard and spoke to Emma. "I think it is such a good idea and I know Richard would find it all very interesting."

Emma looked over at Richard; he didn't seem too enthused about it. Now she thought she knew why Jill was so keen on Emma's family history, something to keep him busy while she was at work. He would have something to work on and Jill would not feel so bad about being the breadwinner while he was 'writing' or maybe she was being cynical. However, something was worrying her, his smile was too pleasing almost fake, far too handsome for his own good. "I would be interested," Emma said thinking it would be a good way of getting to know him. A cold sweat broke out on her forehead as she put two and two together. I'm going to keep a close eye on you, she thought.

Spring 1940

Emma's mind was constantly filled with thoughts about Nickolas, it had been months and he had not written one word to her. She sat in the kitchen rolling out pastry for Doris lost in her own misery. "War is a terrifying experience Emma; you can't spend all day wallowing in your own problems." Doris knew she was speaking out of turn but she loved Emma like she was her own and knew she needed a good talking to. "The country is going to have to pull together if we are going to survive. Resolve yourself to have no more thoughts on your own feelings. Get a job and join up to help the war effort, that's what we did in the last war; I had a good time as well."

Clarice had an annoying habit of being everywhere and knowing exactly what the servants were saying. "Emma you can do your bit for the war effort but you can do it at home, you do not need to join up to anything."

Emma blamed her mother for Nickolas's desertion of her and was always on the look out to irritate her in any way. "I'm going to volunteer to become a nurse."

"You are most certainly not!" Clarice rallied. "Bounding up wounded men, can you image the mess? Not to mention what they will be like when they are better!"

"Mother, I feel I must do this. We must all pull to together as Doris said."

Clarice glared at her cook, "What ideas have you put in this girl's head."

Doris had gone quiet but Molly who was washing up some dishes came up with a sensible solution.

"Emma you should join the women's land army. Lady Denman is chief and I'm sure your mother will be more than happy to support her," Molly explained. "You can work here and help the war effort. I'm sure Lord Attwood will be very supportive and Lady Attwood." She whispered the last name and gave a short curtsey.

Clarice nodded a stiff reply. "What a good idea," Emma beamed. "Why we could all join and get some of the women in the village to work here as well. I like the idea of being in the fresh outdoors. Thank you Molly."

Emma knocked on her father's office door and entered when she heard him call. "Father I have decided to join the land army, I can work on the farmland we have got here and I can do my bit for the war."

"Well, Emma, my little girl, I am so proud of you, yes you have my full support. Tom was saying only the other day farm hands were leaving, more pay in the army. Yes I think it is a brilliant idea."

Clarice rushed into the office, "Full support? Brilliant idea? Do you know what the land army is, I remember from the last war – it is farming! Emma you will be up to eyeballs in mud and manure!"

"We must do our bit, Clarice," Harold finalised, "Emma you may go."

Emma left the office to tell her sisters of her news, while Harold spoke to Clarice. "I am going into London tomorrow, I have a meeting with Winston, I think he wants a favour."

"Don't tell me anymore, I'm going for a lie down."

Lord Attwood was taken back when he received a note from Winston Churchill; he was a very busy man and could only spare Harold a quick lunch but for what reason Churchill wanted to talk about was beyond him. As soon as the pair sat down to lunch Winston was his energetic self. Rapidly eating and talking at the same time and raising his voice when he got over excited. It wasn't long before the conversation turned to latest news; rumours were many, politicians were increasingly uncomfortable with Chamberlain's leadership. With the end of the meal both breathed in fat cigars, while speaking about the prime minister.

"He still wants peace with that mad man! We cannot tolerate that!" Churchill spoke with contempt. "I am ready to lead, to be prime minister, to take on the challenge and the burden and still they think war is not a necessity and that I am over reacting!"

"Chamberlain will not leave from what I have heard, clings on with his finger nails."

"He is trying to form a government with input from all sides but I doubt Attlee will go for it. Everyone now knows we have to fight a long and drawn out war. No matter who is in charge whether it is him or Lord Halifax – appeasement is no longer an option."

Harold smiled, "Lord Halifax does not want the top job, you're the country's only choice."

"Yes, but will they see it that way?! The house does not want to go down this peace route but they will not back me."

Harold knew why, Winston was a good friend but he also knew how headstrong he could be, often charging into places and situations without taking due care. "Do you think we can win this war?" Harold asked bluntly.

"For our island's sake I hope so! We have left it dangerously late though; I tried to warn people we must get Stalin on side. What did they do but carried on talks with the Germans in an attempt for us to avoid war. They offered them money, have you ever heard of anything so stupid. It sent the worst message to Stalin but I must admit their union did surprise me and with luck it will not last but until then we fight alone. Our only hope is the French and I believe the French army is the best in the world, we have a strong alliance there and with a lot of good fortune we may come through victorious. However, we need a strong leader. We need one who will not give in, no matter how bleak things may look."

"But after what happened in Norway, you can understand..." Harold dared to mention the resent disaster but trailed off when Churchill's eyes lit up.

"This is what I am saying! I give them a great strategy and they wait and wait by that time the Germans had somehow figured out what was happening! If only we had got Narvic, we could have made it through to Finland, fighting the Germans on two fronts, cutting off their iron ore supply. But I suppose that is the sadness of war, you never know what the weather is going to be like and the troops were inadequately trained for it."

This to Harold was an understatement, from newspapers reports the weather in Norway was terrible, freezing and deep snow. The soldiers were not trained for such weather conditions and so they had to be evacuated.

"To win this war we need air power as well as sea power to win battles now and planning every scrap of information we can get we must. Our troops must be well equipped for all situations." Churchill took another long puff on his cigar before continuing, "Men are signing up, lots of them aren't even waiting to be called up, they are so eager to fight. We have to get them trained for all types of fighting, in all types of weather and with many different weapons. If we give them the best training, they will have a better chance of coming home." He put his head down remembering Gallipoli before finishing with, "And I'm ready to lead them to that victory." Harold could see how desperately Winston wanted to redeem himself. He had made mistakes and he was determined not to make another one.

"King George must send for you, all of Great Britain is crying out for you."

"I think his mind is made up on Lord Halifax and Chamberlain will not say any different. Anyway, now for the reason why I wanted to see you; we need training grounds, lots of them. What is going on at your estate?"

"My daughters have joined the land army and will be farming as much of it as they can manage."

"What about the woods and the fields to the left of the estate?"

"Do you want to requisition the house?" Harold panicked.

"No we can put up suitable accommodation in the woods, that way a German plane will not spot our training camp."

"Oh I see, of course. I understand and give my full permission."

Within weeks Emma had signed up and received her new uniform and on the other side of the estate Major Edward Grey met Earl Harold Attwood with a warm hand shake. "It all starts again," the Major said as he surveyed the landscape. "You have a lot of land here sir."

"My family's wealth, I served in the last war, like you. I wanted to stay on in the army but my father died, days before the end and well he wanted me to have this."

"Sir I thank you for letting us use your land."

"I'm sure, I'm sure. Now," continued Harold, "as you know the women's land army will be covering the farmland but this might have to be extended further so we will have to mark out boundaries."

"I will do my best to make sure the soldiers' training does not interfere with the ladies farm work."

Harold showed Major Grey a map of the estate, "This will be your area and if you follow that path," he point to it, "it will lead you into the woods, where several shelters have been put up. They are among the trees, just in case a German should be flying near by. Up here," he pointed near to the house, "is your cottage where you and your wife will be. Do you have any children?"

"Yes, I have two girls, Louise and Harriet. Louise is nine and Harriet is six"

"Just as well you are not fighting with such a young family."

"I suppose." Edward didn't want to start moaning why he was sent here, instead of leading his men out into battle. The war office line was that he had more in touch with the common soldier and will be of more use training them. To Edward though this meant he was still not trusted and they wanted to keep him in his place. Or maybe they thought he would show up other military ranks as he would not be staying in some posh hotel while his men take German bullets. Whatever the reason he told himself not to dwell on it, he had a job to do here.

"I've got three girls myself and two boys, who are serving." Harold continued, while he folded up the map to give to Major Grey, another man joined them. "Ah Lord Attwood, may I introduce you to Sergeant Major Adams, he will be keeping the men in check as well as training them."

"Lord Attwood." Sergeant Major Adams gave a small, stiff bow before making his excuses. "I have seen the shelters; I will now go over the training ground, with your permission."

"Yes of course, please by all means."

Harold watched the Sergeant Major march away from them. "Do not mind him." The Major felt embarrassed, "He is like that with everyone."

Harold shrugged, "I guess he has a lot on his mind, like all of us. Tell you what why don't you and the Sergeant Major come for dinner tonight. We can get to know each other a bit better."

"Lovely, tonight it is." Edward wasn't so sure if Sergeant Major Adams would attend but he hoped he would make the effort, Lord Attwood was a good man. He wasn't in the least bit pompous. More like the jolly old man type, rotund, quite bald and quite short. His patriotic spirit made him seem a bit of a figure of fun. Edward thought his good natured character, could be mistaken for idiocy. He was a gentle soul who somehow had landed on his feet. And if Edward had any doubts Lord Attwood would keep interfering like some ex-officer who thought their knowledge was superior to those who had actually fought, he was wrong. Harold's pride in his country did not transform into an ego of himself. He just wanted to help as many poor souls as he could.

"What are you looking at?" asked Emma. Her mother was looking from the landing window, down on to Harold and the Major chatting.

"Just seeing what he looks like?"

"Does it matter?"

"If I have to have soldiers walking about the place, then I wish them to look smart! But he's in uniform and looks very well turned-out. In fact he is a very handsome chap. Although I expect he is of the lower classes, he does not have the look of aristocracy. However, his shoes are very clean. I guess though that it would be the first thing they teach in military school."

"Do you judge everyone on the state of their shoes?"

"It is a good indication, of where they are in society." Emma rolled her eyes, as Clarice continued talking. "He looks quite young for a Major."

Emma looked down on the gentleman, "He is neither young nor handsome."

Harold called to Emma as she walked past his office door. "Ah Emma, Lady Denman has sent these forms, for any new recruits for the women's land army. Now you have signed up, you have to take it seriously. You can't go bunking off because you live here. I'm paying you not only to help on the land but also to help train the other girls. It's been decided you should train a week with Tom, and then you could train the other girls as you learn new skills from Tom."

"I think it might be better if he teaches all of us. I'm never going to learn everything in a week."

"He will only show you what needs doing now, he wants you to take it seriously though, so no whinging. Tom doesn't like the thought of the girls running the farm; it is your job to show you can handle the work. Make me proud, it took all my effort to persuade him to teach you. Now Emma you have to prove me right and put your all into this." Emma sat looking up at her father's eager face and watched as he got up from his chair, put his hands behind his back, paced the floor a little and then started on the war speech. "You have the responsibility of feeding England. You will be their Captain, their Major, their leader, through the wind, rain, snow, ice in winter and the hot burning sun of the summers. No one is saying it's going to be easy, oh no, don't be fooled by the posters but it will be satisfying when you... mmm... you know crop something. Anyway you are entering the army, so make me proud!" he repeated.

Emma had stopped listening long ago. "Emma? Emma?".

"Yes Father. I will try my hardest, I promise. May I get ready for dinner now?"

"Go, tomorrow you will have a rude awakening."

Dinner came with the introduction of the Major and Sergeant Major Adams, to the rest of the family. On closer inspection Clarice was right; Major Grey was a very good looking man. His soft brown hair was parted perfectly in a straight line at the side of his head. His pale blue eyes twinkled with boyish mischief. He was tall, lean and his manner was polite. His deep seductive voice matched the masculinity of his uniform. Sergeant Major Adams on the other hand was older, in his fifties and severe looking. He made no conversation nor did he try to participate in others. His mood was generally out of humour but tonight even more so. To him nothing was worse than being civil to people born with a silver spoon in their gob. It angered him even further when jokes were made, how could anyone laugh at a time like this when young men will have to face the horrors of war. Major Grey on the other hand was enjoying the company immensely, especially of Lord Attwood. Any pre-conceived judgement on his intellect had now vanished; to Edward's surprise he spoke a lot of sense. He also particularly enjoyed gazing at Lord Attwood's youngest daughter. He saw her blush when he first entered the dinner room and now shyness had got the better of her. In an attempt to tease Emma, he caught her eyes with his. It felt like a lighting bolt had just shot through her, she almost recoiled in her chair. "I hear you plan to join the land army with your sisters; I did not expect that, I am genuinely impressed with such sentiments," Edward said, trying to keep the humour out of his voice, he knew they would not last the day.

Before Emma could answer, her mother squealed with delight. "Oh do not encourage her! How are you ever going to find yourself a husband when you are covered in mud?"

"We have to do our patriotic duty. I'm looking forward to earning my own money."

"Emma, women from this family do not earn money, they marry it."

"As you know that did not work out for me," Emma said mournfully.

Clarice turned her attention to the Major. "What about you, sir, how did you come to be a Major?" Clarice continued her interrogation.

"I joined up in 1915, nearing the end of the first war, mainly because my brother had done so; he's three years older than me. I was 14 but by that stage they didn't care what age you were as long as you were willing to fight. I lied to the recruiting office and before I knew it I was on my way to war. My first battle was Gallipoli. How I survived that I will never know!"

"Such a dreadful time," Harold said, remembering his own horrors of the last war.

"I was lucky really; we were in rowing boats, which dropped us off at the bottom of a steep cliff. We couldn't carry up heavy artillery equipment but we had our guns and thankful the Turks were not expecting us. They thought we would not climb the cliff so it wasn't properly manned."

"It was a sad story for many others!" Sergeant Major Adams piped up, but Edward ignored him and continued.

"Anyway after the war I stayed on and worked my way up. I was lucky my head of divisions, Sergeant Manners, wrote some wonderful reports on me and so here I am."

"They wouldn't let you fight either! I told them I'm as fit as anything!" said Harold taking another sip of wine and going red with it.

"I would go, but I'm glad to be training the lads, it is important they know what they are facing and my experience is extensive." Emma looked into his eyes once again but now they were dead and he looked straight through her.

Outside it was still cold, they had had the worst winter for many years and even the English Channel had frozen. She then groaned inwardly remembering she would have to be up at five tomorrow morning in the dark and freezing cold. At least, she consoled herself with the knowledge she would not be thinking about Nicholas.

When Emma's attention returned to the dinning table they were still talking about war. "Good training that is exactly what they need. Good survival skills. I know that is what Churchill wants," Harold said.

"Churchill! What does he care?" Sergeant Major Adams raised his voice. "He just throws men at a badly thought out idea and then is baffled as to why it didn't work! That is all he thinks the lower classes are good for!"

Harold shook with rage and excitement, it had been a long time since he lost his temper. "Who do you think you are? To be making such a false statement!" After the defeat at Gallipoli, Winston resigned from his post and became an ordinary solider. No one knew the importance of life and the difficulties of war better than Churchill." Before Sergeant Major Adams could retaliate, Clarice stepped in, to Edward's relief.

"What is your wife like Major Grey?"

The Major laughed, "Always the centre of attention."

"And your daughters?"

"The same!"

Clarice didn't think much of this. "Well I look forward to meeting them," she lied. Her attention turned on Emma. "You haven't eaten much; you will have to keep your strength up, if you insist on digging up half the countryside."

Emma had not had much of an appetite for weeks and she knew she was looking unattractively gaunt.

Edward could see Emma's sadness; he could sense her isolation. He now felt bad for teasing her and wanted to put things right. "I do think, Miss Attwood, you are very brave and courageous to be taking on such a hard job."

"Thank you sir, I will certainly try my best."

"She's a good girl and very bright as well, she will have no problem." Lord Attwood beamed at his daughter.

The evening ended with kind words but very little in common, Clarice hoped that now the initial hospitalities were out the way she would now have very little to do with them.

It was not a good start to the day; Emma had overslept and had to quickly dress herself in her smart new uniform, brown breeches, white shirt and a green jumper. Very fetching she thought. She made her way towards the outhouses to meet the farmer, Tom Briggs. "Now Lassie, this ain't gonna be easy. I am not gonna let you idle about in the field all day chewing on a piece of grass, and don't be running off if you get a bit of mud on your breeches. This is 'ard graft, you will be doing men's work, I don't want no whinging girl."

"With all due respect sir, I'm here to learn, not to be insulted."

"See! You're too sensitive! Now toughen up, this is a man's job and if we have to use women then so be it, but it don't mean I have to like it."

"Fine then! Then let's bloody get on with it!"

"More like it." They stood in a small courtyard garden, which could be accessed by the kitchen. Emma liked it very much, it caught the sun in the afternoon and you could smell the heady scent of herbs Molly grew on the windowsill. "This morning I want you to dig up all the roses and the hedges in between them. When that is cleared fork fresh manure into the soil and then we can plant some vegetables."

"Yuck, I'll smell!"

"It has to be done, need to keep the soil rich."

"Do I have to dig up this small garden, it is so pretty. Why can't I just plant them in a field?"

"Are you going to argue with me on every job I ask you to do?"

"It's just I thought I would be on a tractor ploughing the land."

"Oh yes and how many time's 'ave you been driving a tractor?" Emma was quiet. "I'm asking you to do this because your 'ouse hold will need feeding and it will be better if the 'ouse has its own supply without dipping into the farm's produce. Last year we had a terrible winter meaning we didn't grow as much as we needed. So the more we plant the more we will 'ave to harvest. Plus this will help you to learn on a small scale. Different vegetables attract different bugs you 'ave to learn how to prevent that."

"Alright I will get on with that." Taking her fork Emma ripped out rose bushes. Straight away her hands were cut up from the thorns and after pulling up just three rose bushes, she was feeling tired. She looked around at the beautiful square garden, where rows of roses and privy hedges met and intertwined. All of it would have to be taken up so they could feed themselves. It was just another stark reminder that even the small pleasures in life, had no place in wartime Britain.

Emma worked hard and by the end of the morning, she had pulled up most of the roses bushes, when Tom came back. "Good job, now these hedges will be tricky because the roots are so deep. You will have to dig trenches all along here, make sure it is deep and then hopefully we can rip it up by placing a fork underneath the root. Emma was feeling exhausted, the thought of her now having to dig huge trenches was a nightmare. Tom got his shovel, he could see how tired she was but she wouldn't say that to him. "When this is all complete and we can put the wooden slants around these beds, and then you will see beautiful green shoots springing out of the mud in a few weeks time. That is when you feel all that hard work was worth it."

"Why do we have to move these hedges, could we not just plant around them?"

"We need the space and anyway when you have to do land clearance you will come up against a lot worse than a few hedges."

Emma put her hand to her head and groaned inwardly, 'what have I let myself in for?'

At the end of the day, all the rose beds were clear, tomorrow they would make up the beds for the vegetables to be grown. "I will then tell you what you need to plant where," Tom explained to her.

"Do vegetables need to be planted in alphabetical order?"

"No! Silly girl, let me show you the green house." It was half five and Emma who had been working since six that morning, with only a light lunch, was staving. She really did not want another lesson but followed him into the greenhouse.

"These are tomatoes, in between the tomatoes we have marigolds planted, this should deter white fly from ruining our crop, understand?"

"I think so."

"You look shattered, go on off you go. Be up early tomorrow, we have a lot that needs doing!"

When morning came, Emma's body ached; all her muscles felt stiff, every joint in her body caused her a small twitch of pain. Her uniform was put on in agony and her breakfast was eaten in a hurry because she had overslept again. When she did make it outside to meet Tom, he was not impressed.

"You will 'ave to be here by five not waking up at five."

"Sorry, what needs to be done today?"

"Planting, first we 'ave to plant these little plants which I had sown last year and kept in the greenhouse so the frost wouldn't get to them. They can now be taken out of the wooden trays and planted into the soil. Now these are the vegetables," he pointed out each different one, showing her what the leaves looked like; to Emma they all looked the same. "Here we 'ave swedes, squashes, lettuces, beetroot, brussel sprouts and leeks, these can be planted now just dig a small hole in the ground and label where you have put each plant." Tom continued over the other side of the small garden. "Over here, is where we will sow the carrots, turnips, potatoes, courgettes and cabbages. That can also be done today, seeds can go straight into the soil, these vegetables can handle the cold but you will have to thin the weaker ones out so the strongest can grow big and have enough space to do so. Just keep your eye on it."

He then went over to the kitchen window, "Over here on either side of this window, I will put up two trailers and grow broad and runner beans. Now on the beans there may be black fly, if that happens take off the tip of the plant."

Emma dug holes, so many inches apart and so many inches deep, as Tom had told her for each different variety of vegetable. The tasks were completely daunting to her and now the reality had hit her she panicked on whether she would remember all the information Tom was giving her.

By the end of the day everything was transformed, Molly was thrilled she had her own kitchen garden, filled with her herbs and vegetables, fruits and pulses. Emma was thrilled too, tired and achy as she was feeling, she was proud of herself. Tom was right it was hard work but worth it. "I guess the hard work is over with now, just a case of waiting for nature to take its course." Emma thought she could relax.

"Not at all. Animals tomorrow and you can meet Joe, he works with me. He will show you how to deal with pest control. That is foxes, moles, rabbits, rats and mice." Tom could see the panic etched across Emma's face. "Do not worry, remember you will have many girls to do as you say, you can leave the 'orrible jobs to them. The point is that you will 'ave to teach them while I'm trying to get orders out. Joe will be here to help you through if you need it." Despite his reluctance to take on Emma, she had not complained and had worked hard. She had proven the job of second in command on the farm had gone to the right person.

Only midweek and Emma had had enough but there was no way she was giving in and proving Tom right.

"Animals, now the bulls are dangerous; they will gore you if you ain't alert. Pigs and poultry 'ave to be fed and eggs have to be collected and the cows 'ave to be milked daily. You also have to make sure they are all in good health, cows can get mastitis, so you need to know the symptoms. Do you know how to take the temperature of a cow?" He smiled when he asked that. Emma shook her head. "You 'ave to stick a thermometer up the cow's backside. They also need to be moved from one field to another so not to overwork the land. Sheep have to be checked for footrot and have their wool sheared in the summer. Remember that when sheep have offspring, it's called that for a reason because it happens in the spring. Nature is all about timing, you might get bored of waiting or lazy but remember starvation can kill a lot more than a bomb. It is vital you stay on top of your chores."

Tom brought it home to her how important farming would be, while war lasted. People need food to keep the country going.

"That field is to be ploughed. So what I want you to do today is to move the cows, to the west side of the farm."

"Where?" Emma was confused.

"See the cows? Move them out of that gate and along the path to that field over there," he pointed, "nearer the barn, in case it rains."

"Rains? It is cold but we have sun, the sky is clear, it's not going to rain!"

"I can sense rain in the air, get those cows moved today."

Emma looked out at the herd, "How in the hell am I going to move them?"

"You will soon get the hang of it. Go on, I 'ave work to do."

Joe was just finishing grooming the horses when he saw Emma standing in the field trying to push a cow forward without any success. "Do you want some help?!" he laughed at her.

"I'm fine!" she lied.

Taking pity he walked over to her. "This is not an easy job, but if you stay one side I'll stay the other and slowly but surely they should start to move."

"How long have you been working here?" Emma asked amazed, she had never seen him and he was so skilful at the job, a few yells and the cows were walking forward.

"I've always worked here, it is nice to know I made such a big impression on you!"

"Sorry, I don't mean to be rude."

"That's alright, I never expected you to be taking up such jobs as this. Most of the blokes are signing up for the army, so we are going to need you womenfolk to keep this country going."

"Are you signing up?"

"Next year. I'm here to keep an eye on the girls. A hard job but someone has to do it." He smile and winked at Emma. "Anyway I think I am of more use on the farm than I would be on a battlefield."

As they neared the west side field, the last cow was pushed in through the gate. "Wasn't so hard, was it?" Emma was astonished, it had been very difficult! Every time a cow had wandered off Joe and the other work hands fell about laughing. Emma had to run back several times into another field to retrieve it and then it didn't want to move, despite all her yelling.

"Now I will show you how to tack up a horse to a cart. You will need the carts when you are harvesting the crops." Emma loved horses, she had been riding ever since she could remember; she thought this would be easy but again she was wrong. The horse did not want to reverse into the cart, despite all Emma's pleading.

"No you have to yell at it, show it who's boss."

Emma was surprised, as she yelled and swore at the horse, in the end it did as she commanded. The horse was so used to the men that she needed to order it about like she was one.

Soon came the job Emma was dreading, pest control. "Rabbits are the worst; eat the crops and digging holes everywhere, ruining the roots. At harvest time though, once the corn has been cut it is easy to spot them, no where to hide. It is a good day for hunting and a good dinner on the table too."

"Are they really that destructive?" Emma was hoping she could avoid killing the fluffy little bunny rabbits.

"Yes, what comes first us or them? This is about survival. They don't know Hitler will try to starve us to death. They don't understand the art of war. It's nature, life's circle and anyway you like eating rabbit don't you?

"Yes I suppose so."

"Well then, if you can eat it, you can kill it."

"I have never fired a shotgun before and they are such fast creatures and so small."

Joe grinned slightly sadistically, "You do not need to worry, we will be breaking their necks with our hands. It may sound harsh but it is quick."

"I can't do that, I can't kill a defenceless animal," she cried.

"If old Briggs hears you like that, you would have proven him right. Now come on, pull yourself together. This is war no time for tears, toughen up."

They walked across the field slowly, keeping their footsteps light. Joe pointed down to say he had found a burrow. "Stay here and be ready," he whispered to her.

"Why, where are you going?" she whispered in panic back to him but he ignored her. He looked for another hole. When he found it, he put a hose down into the burrow and started to gas the rabbit out. Emma at the other end was getting nervous, as quick as a flash the bunny stuck his head up.

"Grab it!" Joe yelled. Emma went to dive on it but the thing leapt at her, knocking her backwards. Joe fell about laughing. "It's not easy."

"Sorry, it was just too fast and I wasn't expecting it to move so forcefully."

"We can try again; there will be plenty more where that came from. Let's get out of this rain."

By the end of the week Emma's head was spinning, there was so much to do and all needed to be done at certain times. Different implements and machinery to get the hang of, so much to know about how to plant and treat animals and now she would have to teach all of this to the girls, most of whom were from the city, only a few from the village signed up.

For every field Lord Attwood agreed to have ploughed up, he would get two pounds per acre. Each girl over eighteen got thirty-two shillings. Life had changed dramatically for Emma but she kept repeating to herself the land army motto – Stick with it!

2009

Emma excitedly put tea and cake in her conservatory and waited for her niece to arrive. She had lived with her niece for four months until the decorating was finished in her bungalow. The pair were always close but found their bond strengthen and now came closer to a mother-daughter relationship. From her very first memories, Aunt Emma had always been there, encouraging and caring for her. She loved her aunt's company and made it a ritual to have a chat every week on a Thursday afternoon.

Emma greeted her niece warmly. "My dear, you are looking so very well! How are you and tell me how are my great nephew and niece?"

"I'm well and as for the terrible two, I think they are ok. Both seem to be enjoying university a little too much, all change next year though when they come back. Then they will have to deal with the real world."

"They are good kids, just as well I moved out otherwise it would be such a squeeze!"

"We would have made room." Elizabeth made it clear Aunt Emma would always be welcome in her house. "What about you? Have you settled in here?"

"Yes I am happy to be back in the neighbourhood."

"You never said all that much after you viewed the house. Did you remember anything new?" Elizabeth could not remember all that much about the house, she had no attachment to it, but her mother's memory. She would encourage Emma to tell funny stories of the sisters growing up.

"Everything has changed, inside and out but I can still sense my mother and father, Bernie, your mother, William and Jack. Everywhere I turned; I remembered things, things I had long forgotten. I remember when mother took Bernadette into London for a day's shopping and to meet her snotty friends. Both Maria and I were very jealous and Jack and William called her Bernie bossy boots. Being the eldest you see of course she was favoured and in my defence I was only five at the time. We dug a hole in the garden and filled it with water, leaves, grass and twigs. Then put the tuff back over the hole and placed a chair on top." Emma laughed with that childish mischief. "When Bernadette came in we said 'oh you poor thing come and sit in the garden and relax after such a busy day out.' She went straight through and covered her beautiful clothes in mud!"

"How naughty of you all, I can't believe it!"

"Yes mother gave us the slap of our lives but it was worth it. When I walked past the entrance of my father's office I half expected to see him sitting at his desk, through the crack in the door. That is what set off the memory; I could see myself waiting outside for him to talk to me. I had never seen my father so angry. It was cruel but so funny."

Elizabeth laughed, she could just see them doing it. "Do you think it was for the best then, coming back here?"

Emma shrugged, she hadn't decided yet. It had surprised her how raw everything still was, how emotionally difficult to confront her past, in fact she still had yet to confront it.

Elizabeth changed the subject, "You should tell her who you are, give her the chance to decide."

"It is not as easy as that. Something is going on and if I start saying oh by the way I am your grandmother, it will cause even more upset."

"Why, what is going on? Have you had contact with her?"

"Yes, not on purpose, events took over."

"Alright so what has happened that restricts you from telling the truth?"

"I'm not sure as yet, I have no proof but I think an affair is going on, a very dangerous affair that could hurt all people involved."

"What are you going to do?"

"I haven't got a clue, I want to help my granddaughter but telling the truth will create more problems than it solves and what if she doesn't thank me for it. Which I doubt she would, it means I will never get the chance to know her."

"But what if this affair destroys her and you could have stopped it."

"Only if they are found out, the affair might just fizzle out. No one will be the wiser."

"You are too beautiful," Richard said, while stroking her face.

"You're not so bad yourself," she giggled. She loved to be with him and felt she had a power over him; he simply could not resist her. She remembered how his face looked when she first accosted him. The shock, surprise and excitement she evoked in him, was overwhelmingly pleasing. His eyes had scanned her body with dark attraction and she knew she had caught him.

"Why did you marry Mrs Granger?" He winced whenever Matilda mentioned her, she was his wife and he loved her dearly and to him she was known as Jill, nothing else. When Matilda called her Mrs Granger it brought home how serious this relationship was and how much trouble he could get into.

"Let us not dwell on my reasons for marriage."

"You can't love her, she is hardly anything special."

"Can you not insult her while you are in her house? Why do you have to ruin everything?"

"Why do you always have to stick up for her?"

"Why do you have to insult her? Isn't it bad enough you're sleeping with her husband?"

"I am not the one cheating. You are. I owe her nothing."

"Nothing? She has been your teacher these past six, seven years. It was her who convinced your father to let you board and that she would look after you and all so you could get away from your aunt."

"I didn't ask for her help."

"You really are a brat," he said reaching for his shirt. Matilda loved to get him riled up.

"If you don't like me I could always go." She walked behind him slowly, and lent over his back to kiss his cheek and neck.

"One of these days, your seductive kisses will not work on me. You need to get back."

"I like to be here with you."

He was about to argue when a knock came at the door. "Stay here. What if it is Jill?"

"Why would she knock? Idiot," she giggled

"This isn't funny," he said pulling on his trousers. "What if they want to come in?" Matilda wriggled out of his grip.

"Ignore it."

"I can't what if it is Jill and she has forgotten her keys?"

"Why don't you just see who it is?"

"Go out the back door and make sure you are not seen, keep your head down." He waited until he heard the back door shut then walked to the front door. As he looked through the spy hole he sighed out heavily. "It's the old woman," he whispered, to an empty room, before opening the door.

Emma stood glaring at Richard who had answered the door with an open shirt and his trousers half done up.

"Have I caught you at a bad moment?"

"Just woken up, can I help you with something?"

"I photocopied this for you, it's my family tree."

"Thank you it will come in handy," he said trying to conceal his fast racing heart and breathlessness.

"Do you want me to tell you a bit about it, over a nice cup of tea perhaps?"

"I would love to but could we arrange it for another day? I have a bit of a headache, night out with the lads. You know."

"Yes of course, I understand. You know where I am if you wish to see me."

"Thank you Miss Attwood. I will be in touch."

As he shut the door, he saw Matilda still standing there. "Matilda?"

"I left something upstairs." He walked back upstairs behind her.

"You should have left what if the old woman had come in?"

"I'm sure you would think of something."

"What did you forget?"

"My folder." It was sitting on the dressing table next to the wardrobe, which was slightly ajar.

"What are you doing? Put that stuff back."

"I'm just looking." She was going through all of Jill's clothes. "When can I see you again?" she asked carelessly.

"I'm not sure; I have work to be getting on with. I want to start writing that book for Jill and I won't have much time for you, but I'll call you."

"Why don't you just leave your wife? I have money, we could live together, you could write any book you like."

"That will go down well with your father. Anyway I am a happily married man. You wouldn't want the world to know what you have been getting up to."

"I don't care. I want everyone to know that we are together."

"Ah Matilda grow up, I can't deal with you when you are like this. Be sensible, this is just a bit of fun, understand?" Matilda eyes started to weep. "Go back to school and while you are there learn how to be an adult."

"Why can't you love me?"

"What?" This came out of nowhere. "I am married, I love someone else. We have fun though, don't we? You knew right from the start, that's all it was going to be."

"I hate this house, I hate that ring on your hand and I hate your wife! If this is the way you are going to treat me I'll just walk away."

"Fine, if that's what you want."

"Why are you doing this?"

"Doing what? You want to leave so leave." She broke down in a hard sob. "Don't get hysterical, it makes you look unhinged."

"What! Why do you hate me?! You say the most horrible things to me but as soon as your boring wife leaves you alone you are back begging me to see you."

"Don't mention my wife! How many times do I have to ask you not to mention her?"

"I'll tell her, I'll tell her everything!"

"Everyone will call you a slut! That is what you are, throwing yourself at a married man! I have the text messages." He lied as her cries were getting louder.

"I love you. Please forgive me, I won't breathe a word. Please tell me you love me too." In her head she was sure he did love her, she had formed a fantasy of the man she wanted to be with, not the man he was and these words were not the words he would have said to her, they were spiteful and cruel.

"You are pathetic; get your folder and go."

"When I walk out that door I'm not coming back."

"You will, you love me," he mocked her. He didn't like what he was doing but he was angry with her, it was she who threw herself at him and put his marriage in jeopardy. He loved his wife dearly but lust was a trick and he was well and truly duped. He watched her slam the door behind her. He always hated the way he felt after she left but today his guilt was stronger not only had he betrayed his wife but Matilda had expressed an emotional dependency on him. He had no idea how he would free himself from this suffocating affair.

Summer 1940

Tom had decided to let Emma take the Saturday off; she had been working so hard. He didn't want to be going easy on her but he also didn't want her being worked to exhaustion. Emma lay in bed and enjoyed being lazy, when she heard her mother scream with delight. "They are back!"

Slipping on her dressing gown, she made her way downstairs. Maria came and kissed her sister, "Well what do you think?" She gesticulated over to Harold who was holding a tiny baby. He had taken Maria to the hospital and had waited outside for all the forty-three hours, he looked shattered but his second grandchild and his first female grandchild lay happily in his arms, sleeping. He put the little girl in Emma's arms. "I have named her Elizabeth," Maria said, "I hope one day soon we will have a Margaret to join her," she joked.

"She is a little dear." Emma cooed over the baby while stoking her soft cheek. The baby opened her tiny eyes a bit, held on to Emma's finger, and then shut them again. "Congratulations."

"Emma this is the first time you have held a baby and it has not cried!" Clarice announced.

"Mother!" Maria said angrily. "They are obviously twin souls."

Emma looked down on the sleeping baby, still holding on to Emma's finger, "She really is a little dear."

Sunday morning, Emma got ready for church, her mother had told her not to wear her uniform but it was so filthy anyway she did not mind. In the lane leading up to the church was Major Grey and his family, walking slowly along. Harold was quick to shout them a greeting and they stopped to wait for the Attwood's to catch up with them. Edward then introduced his family to them all, "Lord and Lady Attwood may I introduce my wife and two daughters. Scarlett my wife and Louise and Harriet, my daughters."

"How do you do," Clarice said with all the condescension she could muster.

"How do you do, Lady Attwood. I must say what a handsome hat you are wearing."

"Oh thank you dear and your dress is so very smart."

"Thank you; I felt I must wear tweed in the country."

"I could not agree more! I am always telling my girls that they should wear more tweed."

"Yes, Edward tells me, your girls are joining the land army, quite surprising."

"I know! They are going to be up to their necks in mud, I am quite ashamed of them."

"No tweed for them."

"No indeed. Still they are all adults and if that is what they wish. I suppose it is good for my older girls, what with their husbands going off and fighting in the army. I'm sure the work will take their minds of the distressing reality of it all. I do pity them so I do not argue."

"Yes, I am very lucky Edward got this job here. The village it so basic and the people so plain, nothing like London people but at least we have each other."

"I know what you mean," Clarice lowered her voice. "Not the most interesting of people. That is putting it kindly. We only used to use this house as a summer retreat, normally we would be in London but with all this war talk over the past two years, Harold decided we should make this our permanent residence."

"I am so glad I met you Lady Attwood, I feared I would not get along with anyone."

"My dear I think we will be good friends."

While Lady Attwood and Mrs Grey were gossiping, Major Grey came and walked beside Emma. "How has your first few months been?"

Emma blushed slightly that he would take any interest in her. "It has been very tiring but rewarding."

"It is a good job you are doing, very worth while. And are you happy to lead your troops into battle?"

"Hardly! I'm useless!" she laughed nervously.

"Nonsense. You will be an excellent leader, a Major like me soon enough."

"You are teasing me."

"No, I would not tease you, I admire you to much." He gave her a smile before walking away.

In church Emma sat in front of him, her family always took the first pew. When the Vicar was saying prayers for the war to soon be over, Emma bowed her head and tried her hardest to pray for all the soldiers' safety, especially her brothers and brothers-in-law. To her though there was only one man she could think about and that was Nickolas. Over the week of hard work she had not had the time to think of him but in church, a time of contemplation, she prayed with tears in her eyes for his safety. And for some reason, beyond Emma's concious feelings, she prayed she would always love him.

Early Monday morning and Emma met her little army once again, there were only twelve of them but at least they were eager. Both Maria and Bernadette grinned at their little sister; neither of them was taking part today they were just there to listen, so that cut down the numbers to ten. Both of them were thinking that Emma had not listened to a word Tom had said now she was stuck. Far from it, Emma woke up with a clear head and fresh country air in her lungs. Tom stood next to her not saying a word, "This field you are standing in needs to be cleared, all rocks, boulder, branches and trees have to be taken away." She gave clear and precise information how tools and horses would be used to clear the field.

"So let's get started!" Tom walked away pleased, she had listened to what he had told her and with such a big job it would give Emma a chance to observe her girls.

She asked some of the girls what they thought about the uniforms, and got a rather cheeky reply. "I reckon by the time they have got your jumper up and your trousers down they'd be too knackered to do anymore!" Laughter floated on the breeze of the land and Emma felt reassured she was capable of running the farm efficiently.

Harold listened to the wireless in disbelieve. He had been reading the newspapers everyday and as far as he was aware everything in France had been going well. Now the most dreadful and worrying news had been announced. British troops were retreating from France. Churchill's strongest army had been defeated. Dunkirk had fallen. The Nazis lay just beyond the channel. 'Any day now Hitler will invade England, England lost forever,' Harold thought as he fought hard not to cry, 'our beautiful England, no more.' His first concern was his family; he called them all into the office. Emma was the last to join them, she had been out all day in the field enjoying the sun and laughing with the girls. On seeing her father's down crested look, her stomach tightened with fear. She knew something awful had happened. Harold confronted his family while trying to fight back bitter tears to tell them the news of Dunkirk. "France has fallen, the Nazis have invaded, it is only matter of time before England goes the same way. Hitler will invade any day now."

"What will happen to us Father? What about Derek?" asked Bernadette, who was ashamed to hear her question spoken like a child.

"I want you and your sisters, your children and your mother to pack some clothes and get on a ship to America."

"What about you?" Clarice asked aghast.

"I will wait for the boys to return but we will stay and do whatever is asked of us by our country," Harold told her.

"You have said it yourself the war is over there is nothing to defend!"

"Clarice! I will not argue over this. I fought for my country once and by God I will do it again! It is my duty!"

There was a silence, while everyone contemplated the future.

"I want to stay as well," Emma spoke quietly, expecting an argument. "I'm part of an army," she explained. "I'm staying too."

Clarice looked at her daughter's pale face, normally she would have been appalled but she too had so much to fight for, she wasn't going anywhere. "Harold if you are staying then you cannot expect us to leave, Bernadette and Maria will want to wait for their husbands to return and I have our sons to think about. We cannot leave. Anyway I'd like to see a Nazi argue with me!" she said with nervous laughter.

"We couldn't go anyway," Maria said. "We have a duty to our country, as well as to our husbands." She looked at Bernadette.

"Yes, we have got a job to do. How can the men fight on an empty stomach? No, we are most defiantly staying and if anyone tries to stop us I will hit them with my shovel!" Bernadette finished.

Harold turned his back to them and looked out the window, "Normally I would demand you all go but as I feel so strongly about staying and seeing this through to the end, I can see your desire to do the same. We will stay and hope for a victory." Harold choked down his fears, if the Nazis were to invade he was sure the most horrific of crimes would happen to women. He was torn between duty and his family but then Emma started to sing sombrely, 'There'll always be an England'. Each joined in with the tune, knowing what a false statement this could be. In a few days there might not be a country to fight for and England could cease to exist.

Harold listened to his old friend on the wireless; Winston Churchill was asking for volunteers to defend the country if there was going to be a Nazi invasion. Harold gathered all the men in the village, during the day he would train them with anything he could get his hands on. Knives, forks, wooden poles, pots used for helmets, anything. With the help of Major Grey's counsel they all practiced using these implements to the best of their ability. At night they would break into pairs, the cool summer breeze, would help take away the nervous fire in their cheeks. Harold's heart would beat with pounding trepidation; fear would be in his stomach. The imagination would take over when they would walk the fields, trying to listen out for the slightest movement. The fear was German planes would fly overhead and German soldiers would parachute down into the fields where no one would see them. Night and at dawn break these searches would take place and each time Harold would be scared.

In the newspapers it was now being reported Hitler's plan was to starve Britain into submission by destroying the merchant ships by U-boats. Emma's job became all the more important, the war of agriculture wanted more cereals and double the food supply and so with her father's permission more fields would have to be dug up. First though they had to harvest what they had grown that year. It was Emma who drove the binder, round in circles to cut the corn. Tom explained to Emma: "The corn has to be just ripe and dry, you can hear it rustle in the wind, that's when you know it is ready to be cut."

Emma looked up at the huge binder, with its hexagon frame on the side of the tractor. At first it seemed daunting but she soon got used to it. The other girls collected the corn and stacked it in rows to dry it out completely. Each bit of corn had to be bound together and stacked. Each stack had to be made into a wigwam and then placed together in a group of six. Air had to flow through these to dry out the ears of corn, ready for the threshing machine.

Joe had a great time shooting the rabbits that would appear from the corn. It was a wonderful day, extremely hard work, especially for the girls who had to collect the corn, bits of it would stick to their uniforms and horrible stinging nettles would be hiding in it. But no one complained and at the end of the day Molly put on a lovely spread, with sandwiches and cakes. Bowls of strawberries and raspberries, everyone sat out on the field, enjoying the end of a great day. "Who would of thought we would be doing this?" Maria said, while stuffing a cucumber sandwich in her mouth.

"I know, in a way we are very lucky."

"Mother will go mad when she sees the state of us!"

"IT!" Joe yelled, while tapping her on the back, straight away Emma was up and chasing after him. Maria and Bernadette running behind, "Get him we need to show who is boss!" Emma yelled.

All the girls were up on their feet and chasing him over the now bare fields. "No one messes with the land army girls!" they all shouted with fits of giggles as they all pounced on him.

"Alright, enough of that, we still have a busy day tomorrow. Emma get your girls in check." Tom did his usual stern voice but even he had a slight smile on his lips.

The farm had only one tractor and they were lucky to have that. Tom had trained Emma on it so while the other girls had to make sure the chickens eggs were collected, the cows milked and all the animals fed, Emma happily sat on her tractor and ploughed the fields.

It was during one of these ploughing sessions one morning when Emma noticed a man, someone she didn't recognise. He was in uniform. He was walking closer to the house. He looked terrible, Emma still couldn't recognise the face he was too far away but somehow his walk seemed familiar. Fear grabbed her, maybe it was just a solider, saying one or worse both of her brothers had died, or Derek or Henry. All of them had been involved in heavy battle and none of them had heard a word since then. She put her head down and concentrated on the job in hand, bad news could wait.

Doris answered the door to a rather scruffy solider. "Can I help you?" she asked nervously.

"Doris don't you recognise me?"

She scrutinized his face, "Mr Morris?"

"Yes, have I changed that much?"

"I'm ever so sorry sir. I will go and get your wife. Lady Attwood is in the drawing room."

Clarice sat with Scarlett, the two of them in deep conversation, when Derek walked in. "Good God, what in the hell happened to you?" Clarice spoke without thinking.

"It is nice to see you too."

"Scarlett this is my son-in-law, Derek Morris. Where is Henry?"

"We lost contact, that is why I was allowed some time off. To find out if you had heard from him?" He tried to sound reassuring, as if he was in a French hospital or a German prisoner but he had no idea where his dear friend was.

He had waited at the platform and asked every solider, every person who might know something but no details were given. "If you can't find him then it is most likely he has been left at Dunkirk because he was injured," the register office told him.

After a few weeks and still no news on Henry, Derek went to the war office. They had no idea and was still sifting through piles of soldiers details, who had not been accounted for. He had been stationed at the boarders and had asked for a two day leave to check if Henry had been in touch with the family. Permission was granted.

Bernadette came running through the door looking just as mucky as he did. "Oh my darling, what have you been through?"

He managed a sly smile then replied, "hell."

"Can I get you anything? Why didn't you write to me and tell me you were arriving today!"

"I'm afraid it is a quick visit, don't worry," he said looking at his wife's anguished face, "I look a lot worse than I am." Clarice saw this as an understatement; he had tanned skin and the beginning of a beard, he also looked leaner. But she still gave her son-in-law a warm hug to say welcome home.

"Doris!" yelled Clarice on being so near and smelling him. "Draw Mr Morris a bath!"

"I'm sorry about my appearance, but it was a lot worse seven weeks ago when I returned from France." He hoped this would reassure them a bit but they all were flabbergasted at his scruffiness. The war had already taken its toll on his appearance. He was wishing he had thought to have a shave before seeing his wife, she looked so aghast at him but not as much as his mother-in-law.

"That's alright," beamed Clarice, "Doris! Make sure you fill the bath right up. None of that two inches rubbish!"

Later that evening Clarice held a dinner party to celebrate Derek's return. Normally they would not have dinners at night due to night bombing but tonight Clarice was insistent. Harold walked around the house making sure all blackout curtains were pulled tight.

Clarice further insisted on the Greys being there. Bernadette was not happy with such a fuss and with Henry not being with them, she was deeply upset for her sister. Plus she wanted quiet time with Derek. He only had a two day leave and would soon be on his way to the coast, to defend the boarders again.

When Maria saw Derek she looked around hopefully, was Henry with him, she didn't see him; maybe he was called straight to his station. "Have you heard anything of Henry?" Maria asked desperately.

"No, I am afraid not." Not where he had been and now he was slowly giving up hope. "I'm sure he will be in contact as soon as possible."

"Yes I'm sure. Was it really dreadful? Do you think Henry will get home safe?"

"I'm sure he will." He lied, if Henry wasn't accounted for by now then most likely he was prisoner of the Germans or worse.

"How did you get away?" Maria continued to question.

"It was a pleasure cruiser that picked me up," he admitted but he did not want to talk about it in front of her, the more he talked, the more he lost hope. He knew it was most likely Henry was dead. He fought back tears as the shock sunk in. No he would not say any of this to Maria, hope was all she had left, and he would not take that from her.

"Dunkirk, ah how in God's name did you survive that?" Harold asked enthralled.

"Hell on earth. Never in my life…" He stopped himself, not wanting to say anymore for Maria's sake. The fight was so awful, they were ready for the Germans but it all changed. From the north-east they were told, but in fact they were lying in wait to be slaughtered. They came from the south-east, from behind them and pushed them northwards. For days they were pushed back to the coast and had to put up with fierce bombardment from the enemy, left starving, physically and mental exhausted. They had to leave tanks, weapons and in the end men. Just being reminded of it, brought back his shakes. The whole episode seemed to play over and over in his head; it all seemed too real, almost as if he was there again. He could feel the heat of the sun, the trickle of sweat. Constantly being told to pull back and running from base to base waiting for a bullet or a grenade to kill him, like others he had witnessed. Wounded men screaming out in agony begging him to help them. There was only one thing he could do to help them and that was to turn a gun on them and end their nightmare. If only someone could do that for him. They made it to the beach but the bombardment continued, the deafening noise of the bombs and the engines of the planes, would that sound ever leave his ears? He had to remember he was one of the lucky ones, his ship wasn't bombed, he got out of there. He would never tell his wife what he had been through; some things just went too deep to talk about. In two days he would be back to fight.

"Why do you have to leave again, you have done your bit?" Bernadette asked.

"I am fit to fight," he said quietly.

Edward knew what Derek was going through, a desire to be out there doing your bit and a fear that at times was hard to suppress.

77

"I bet you did not expect to see your wife digging her way in the fields?" Scarlett sniggered.

"I am very proud of her, life is not joyous but we must fill our time doing worthwhile activities."

"It is Emma who we have to thank, she is the one working so hard." Bernadette smiled.

"I just do as Tom tells me."

"That isn't true," Edward laughed. "We heard you shouting from the other side of the estate, you were starting to sound like the Sergeant Major."

"Emma you were not shouting," Clarice spoke aghast.

"I'm only joking Lady Attwood. But I have seen Emma in action – very authoritarian."

"I like to get done what I set out to do," she laughed.

"I think you girls have done a marvellous job, three cheers for the land girls." Derek raised his glass.

After dinner, little Arthur, their son came running in, "Daddy!"

"Hello son." Bernadette turned away, tears formed in her eyes, 'how am I going to say goodbye to him again?' she asked herself.

In the late summer the fruit trees had to be harvested. The girls wore their dungarees (which they rolled up the legs to make them shorter) and larked about, singing and gossiping in the warmth of sun. Emma loved this type of work, it was carefree and easy and the girls could enjoy being outdoors without doing anything particularly difficult. The ones who were not scared of heights climbed the trees; Emma would dangle her bare legs from the branches, throwing down the fruit. Their golden skin tingled in the sun, each girl giggled with joy and relished the sense of freedom working the land had brought to them.

Major Grey walked back from the shelters; it had been a long hard day of drills and shouting orders. Now eight of his men were missing, had they decided to run away? Edward didn't think so, two probably but eight! Walking past the fruit trees he could hear high pitched screams of laughter coming from the girls. There they were, eight men with their heads sticking through the bushes, staring at the girls and their bare legs. For a moment Edward didn't say anything himself as he watched Emma jump out of the tree, laughing and tossing an apple into the cart. She fascinated him, on his first introduction of her he had mocked her aspirations of hard labour, now she seemed to had humbled herself to get a better understanding of the world and he could not help but respect her unshakable determination to do so. His admiration for her grew everyday but he tried to tell himself this had nothing to do with her prettiness or youth, she was a person of many qualities and he esteemed her. Finally he remembered why he was there, "Right you lot back to base!"

All the girls turned to the direction where this loud angry voice boomed from, then out of nowhere eight heads popped up from the hedges. The girls now were in hysterics.

"You won't find Hitler 'ere!" one of the girls' teased.

Before the lad could shout his reply, Edward hit him over the head. "Get back to the shelter, your punishment is going to be bad enough without you making it worse."

2009

Emma was surprised when a knock at the door came and saw Matilda standing there, she remembered telling her which road she lived at but not her number. She didn't have time to question her, her face was swollen and her eyes were red. "What is wrong?" she asked but Matilda could not speak. "Come in, can I get you a hot drink, something sweet to calm you down?"

"I've never been wanted in my life," Matilda blurted out, mainly to herself.

"What has brought this on?"

Matilda shook her head. "No, you'll hate me."

"I think you should let me be the judge of that."

Matilda continued to silently sob; she couldn't bring herself to tell the truth, she wasn't even sure why she was there. Why did she need this old lady's comfort? Emma decided to try and engage her on another topic. "How did you find me?"

"I asked a man walking up the road if he knew an Attwood living around here, he pointed me to this house," she explained now calming down.

"What has brought on these tears, what has upset you? Whatever you have done, telling someone is the first way to fix the damage."

"But I have done something so dreadful, it can never be fixed. I thought he loved me. You can't tell anyone or he will hate me even more."

"This wouldn't be Richard Granger, would it?"

"You know! Oh God!" she sobbed.

"I think it is for the best you to keep this to yourself. You must stay away from him. He has made you feel worthless, hasn't he?"

"I love him."

"That maybe so, but he is married and you wouldn't want a broken marriage on your conscience?"

"No, but I know he loves me too, he's just scared."

"Think of Mrs Granger, she knows nothing about this, do you really want to put her through the hurt you are going through."

"Someone has to get hurt, why does it have to be me, why not her?"

"Because she doesn't deserve it, you knew what you were doing when you got involved with her husband, now you will have to face the consequences."

"And that's having my heart broken?"

"I'm afraid so and it is better than the truth getting out. You have got exams to be worrying about. Concentrate on them, education is the key to a good life. You must not see him again, it would ruin your life and others if it got out and you're too good for someone like that, he wasn't thinking about you or his wife. He was thinking about himself and you deserve so much better than that." Despite Emma's warm words, Matilda put her head on Miss Attwood's shoulder and continued to cry. "Don't be too harsh on yourself, we all make mistakes and I promise you this hurt doesn't last forever."

"No one will ever love me."

"You must love yourself first."

Autumn 1940

Tired and muddy, Emma and her sister came in from the darkness. "How is your farming going, dear?" asked her father. It was late and they were exhausted.

"We are managing to stay on top of it, but with the eight new recruits there is so much to do. Joe is helping out a lot, we split the new girls into two groups, he took one and I the other."

"I was watching Joe's group as we were pulling up the potatoes, when this rat came along. The girls screamed so loudly," Maria explained, "when Joe grabbed it by the throat and broke its little neck."

"All the girls screamed and Tom, who was standing nearby checking the quality of the potatoes, went mad telling them if they can't do anything but stand around screaming, he would hand the jobs to someone else," Bernadette joined in.

"Look at the state of you three and on my birthday!" yelled Clarice, who had just come from the conservatory. "Major and Mrs Grey are here, what will they think?" Edward and Scarlett both stood behind her.

"We would probably think they have been busy, rolling about with the pigs," Scarlett said with a hint of sarcasm. "They certainly smell like they have been." The Major quickly stepped in before Emma could retaliate.

"Emma I wanted to thank you for not lodging a complaint about those men."

"What men?" Clarice asked.

"Oh a few weeks ago some boys were being boys," Emma put it discreetly. "It was nothing and it gave all of us a good laugh." She smiled at Edward. "I'll just go and wash." She watched the Major slip his arm around his wife before she left. A conscious feeling of jealousy raged in her as she threw herself on to her bed exhausted, Scarlett was perfect, beautiful blonde curls, a slim waist and pouty red lips, that looked incredibly sophisticated and grown up. She couldn't explain her feelings but she wanted to look just as beautiful. Getting up, Emma ran an eye over all her dresses, 'I have to look stunning' she thought, 'overwhelmingly beautiful'. She was the last to use the bathroom after both Bernadette and

Maria had finished. She chose a dark blue silk dress and did her make-up, so it was a subtle elegance that made a dramatic change from her normal appearance. When Emma returned the transformation was amazing. Edward's eyes smiled with delight on seeing her.

"Oh Emma that is much better, you look very pretty," her mother said approvingly.

"You are unrecognizable Emma," Scarlett said, and Emma noted her flash of irritation with deep satisfaction.

They all sat down to dinner, again Emma was the main topic of debate.

"Well I think they are being very brave, taking on such hard work." Emma could hear her father's voice thunder across the dinning table.

"All that mud! Not quite what I had in mind for my girls," Clarice repeated her sentiments.

"Mother, our men are doing there bit, so we must do ours!" said Bernadette

"Why can't you just knit?" Clarice and Scarlett felt they were now doing their bit by knitting in the local village hall with the other ladies living in the village.

Emma was too tried to defend her opinions, but she was proud of her sisters trying in vain. "Because this nation needs food, with the men fighting for our freedom, we need to keep this country strong!"

"Here, here!" Harold beamed.

"It's unseemly and I do not like all that time Emma is spending with that scruffy lad."

The Major raised his eyes to Emma; it was the first time he wanted to read her respond in her face.

"He is just a friend," she clarified. He felt relief she had shown no hidden feeling for the lad. He noticed while staring at her, she was a very pretty girl and one with so much integrity; he wondered how Clarice was her mother.

"Joe is a good lad and soon he will be fighting for his country. He could of laughed at me and watch me struggle in the fields but he didn't. He came over and taught me. He deserves our respect."

"Our respect? I know what he got up to with the daughter of Mr Benning. I will not discuss it at the dinning table but you better watch his hands!"

83

"He has been a perfect gentleman and Laura Benning is known as a flirt." Wanting to stop the conversation Clarice turned on all of them.

"If you three continue like this you will lose your looks, being out in all sorts of weather. I dread to think what it will do to your skin. Emma you will never get a husband with your skin looking like a piece of leather. As for you two," she looked at Bernadette and Maria, "do you think your husbands will want to come back to two old farm hands."

Maria put her head down, she still had not heard from Henry. A pang of guilt went through Clarice and quickly stopped talking.

"A girl should stay pretty, until her man comes home," Scarlett said ignoring the awkwardness. It really was the most stupid of comments made. "Well Emma, when you get bored of digging, you could do a bit of baby sitting for us." She smiled and then turned back to Clarice, "I do just love to go to a dance." It was like the war, wasn't taking place for her.

"Yes, who cares if Hitler invades, as long as we can waltz?" Emma's catty reply hung in the silence of the dining room before Clarice spoke again.

"Emma is useless with children; she can't even look after her own nephew and niece."

"I will be too busy working anyway," Emma piped up, feeling incredible irked by Mrs Grey, who refused to take Emma's dedication seriously.

After dinner, there were drinks in the main lounge, Scarlett and Clarice spoke of all the gossip in the village. "Some of those village girls, well you have never seen anything like it. They are always after my boys, always out for what they can get. And now Emma is mixing with them too, I hope she doesn't pick up their bad habits."

Emma ignored her mother's loud comment and went to take a seat away from the family near the book case and flipped the pages of one. Major Grey came and sat down next to her, "You look very nice this evening."

"Thank you. I felt I needed to make an effort," she laughed nervously.

"Why is that?" he asked her, staring into her eyes for her response. A flirtatious smile played on his lips, which she copied back but did not verbally answer.

"I'll leave you to your book." He gave her a quick smile before rejoining his wife.

Emma watched him walk over to her father. He often spoke to Harold on interests in Europe and never spoke out of turn, even when they disagreed. "Our brilliant pilots have inflicted heavy losses on the German air force."

"The Luftwaffe outnumber our air force, and I do not think Hitler will give up so easily."

"There is no way he can continue losing planes and men. It will not be long before he has to change strategy. Our boys have proven who has control of the skies."

"I hope you are right Sir, but the odds are not in our favour."

"When has that ever stopped us giving it our all?"

Scarlett noticed Emma staring at her husband, tickled by Emma's little crush; she made her way over to him and put her arm around his waist, watching Emma as she did it. Scarlett wasn't threatened by her, she just didn't like her. She found Emma to be spoilt by her father and disobedient to her mother. A little slap in the face would do her good.

Emma gazed back at Scarlett, her eyes were dancing with the under currents of mockery. Understanding Scarlett's amusement, Emma soon made her explanation of tiredness and went to bed feeling very small.

Emma made her way to the tree where she and Nickolas used to go. She sat down and watched the rapid flowing river, while she tucked into her lunch. Her thoughts whirled about in her mind, he had stuck to his promise, he had not written to her. She was worried about him, like she was worried about her brothers and her brothers-in-law but still in her heart she missed him and desperately wanted to hear from him. Tears formed in her eyes when she thought of their moments together and the happiness he had generated in her. In a moment of fire she berated Nickolas in her mind, 'how dare he put her through this, not even a letter to say he was alright'. Or was this anger, guilt? Try as she might she could not stop herself thinking about Major Grey.

Nickolas looked up at the clear blue African sky. The heat could be unbearable at times but life among army men was what he was looking for. Freedom from his family, a chance for him to prove himself as a man and far removed from the love of his life. For days on end he would not think about Emma but today his army friends had received letters from home. He took out the black and white photo of her and kissed it with a wish that one day she would return that kiss back. But he was now accustomed to war and his first opinions of it were proved right. Life was not guaranteed, he would have to take the heartbreak so Emma had a chance to build a new life without the guilt of betrayal. He wanted her to be happy. He knew that even if he did survive the war and Emma had not met anyone new, she still may not want him back. He prayed to God if that was the truth to kill him on the battlefield, for the thought of holding Emma once again was the only thing keeping him sane.

In a few months they would be pressing forward into Egypt and his mind would once again be occupied with other thoughts but Emma was never far from them.

"I knew you would be back. Come here, you know I don't like it when we fall out." Richard stroked Matilda's cheek. She had tried to avoid her feelings for him but he excited her and when he texted to ask to see him, she could not fight the temptation.

"You have to treat me better or I will leave you for good next time."

"I've got a spare ten minutes, if you want me to demonstrate how sorry I am."

Matilda gave a throaty laugh, "I have to go, I promised Mrs Granger I would attend her class."

Richard grunted. "Her class is pointless, come to bed and keep me warm, that it a lot more rewarding."

"I have changed my mind. I want to be a better person, you were right she has been good to me and I don't want to let her down."

Richard glared at her. "A few days ago you were slagging her off and asking me to leave her, now you would rather hear her lecture you on your behaviour than spend time with me! What has gotten into you?"

"Like I said she has been good to me, I owe her some respect and I promised Miss Attwood I would make more of an effort with my studies."

"Miss Attwood? What has that old bat got to do with this?" Matilda went quiet, she thought about lying but he was already seeing how the situation was unfolding. "Does she know about us?"

"She won't tell anyone, she promised me. Anyway we would deny it, if something did leak out."

"You stupid girl! What did you tell her for?"

"Don't shout at me!"

"Why did you tell her?"

"I didn't mean to but you were being so foul to me!"

"Do you really think the old crow is just going to sit and watch you have an affair with the head-mistress's husband?"

"She thinks it's over between us."

"Well that's alright then!" he said sarcastically. "Matilda I could get into a lot of trouble, as well as lose my wife!"

"I could be your new one."

Richard looked at her eager face, her long blonde hair thrown over her left shoulder. "That's a nice image but no. We agreed this was just meant to be a bit of fun," he said more kindly, "and now everything is a mess."

"Richard please, I love you." Tears filled her eyes.

"Not this again," he sighed deeply. "When you next see Miss Attwood, tell her you were dishonest. That you have some sort of crush on me and you took the story too far."

"No she will think I'm mad."

"Not far from the truth," he said with a flash of pure spite.

She stared at him waiting to see some remorse in his eyes but nothing appeared, he meant what he had said. She ran away in floods of tears, Miss Attwood was right, she should never have gone back.

Winter 1940

Cold and shivering, Emma walked down what seemed like endless rows of celery, knocking frost off them. "You look like you could do with a cuppa!" Joe yelled.

"I can't, we have to do brussel sprout picking next," she was saying as he walked over.

"Here have a sip of this," Joe whispered as he handed her his silver flask full of whisky. "I've signed up, done my medical and all that. I think I will get to train here, with that bloke, what's his name?"

"Major Grey."

"Yeah, that's it and Sergeant Major Adams, the grumpy one. Now when I leave to save the world from the Nazis, make sure you don't run the farm too well, or I won't have a job to come back to."

"You will always have a job here, anyway when this war does end I think Tom will be chasing us girls off the farm. He never seems happy with me."

"Don't you believe it. When old man Attwood came up to him and said girls would be taking over from the men, he turned the air blue. I thought your old man would go mad but he told him, that you would be in charge and that you would work hard. The best of the bunch and you know what, he was right. Tom sees it as well he just doesn't want to admit it."

"Thanks, that's good to know."

"You know I never thought we would be friends, I guess that this war has done something good for us. Otherwise you and I would never have met."

"I'm going to miss you."

"I'll be back; I will have to be I think I've got a few of your girls into trouble." Emma hit him playfully.

"You didn't!"

"Nah, but that Laura is a game bird, Saturday night I'm going to ask her for a dance."

"Good luck," Emma said as he started to walk off.

"I don't need luck and I expect a dance from you as well!" he yelled at her. Emma smiled to herself, 'mother will not like that'.

On every Saturday evening a dance would take place at the 'Barn', the boys being trained by Major Grey would all turn up, as would the land army girls. Emma danced with most of the soldiers, while the Major looked on. Edward thought he should be there to keep an eye on everyone, but he hated it. His wife would join him but would go off dancing with the other men, enjoying the attention.

"This is meant to be fun," Emma joked.

"My wife is making a spectacle of herself."

"She's only dancing."

"I have to work with these men, how can they respect me when they are all chasing after my wife?"

Emma shrugged, "How do you think Joe will get on with his training?" She thought it was best to change the subject.

"You like him, don't you?"

"No."

"You danced with him tonight."

"So? Only to annoy mother, I know it will get back to her."

"Why doesn't she like him?"

"His name would not look good on the family tree. That is the sort of rubbish, my mother believes in."

"Would your mother object if you had a dance with me?"

"I do not know about her, but I object."

"On what grounds?" he asked bemused.

"You are using me to make your wife jealous."

"I am asking you because I want to dance with you, so please would you do me the honour of having this dance?"

"So long as you smile, you can't continue looking grumpy." He smiled his open smile and stepped onto the dance floor.

The music started, they came together, hand in hand, her heart was beating faster and she could feel her cheeks flush. His arm was right around her waist and he held her firmly to him. No words were spoken, just a meeting of eyes. Emma could not help the attraction she felt towards him, being in his arms was something she would savour for the rest of her life.

A few days later at breakfast on Tuesday morning, there was a knock on the front door, Doris answered it and brought in a telegram for Mrs Appleby. Harold was quick off his chair as the letter was handed to Maria. "Don't open that, I'll do it," he said hoping that if he could read it first it might ease the blow for his daughter.

Maria gave it to him, she started to rock herself backwards and forwards. "No please God, no. Please Papa tell me he is in a prison of war, please say injured and coming home. Please tell me he is alive." Cold tears ran down her checks, she could tell from her father's crumpled face what the news was but still she could not bring herself to believe it.

"I'm so sorry, my darling girl. Henry is dead."

"How do they know it's him? They might have got it wrong," she said, holding on to any hope she could reach.

"No, my dear he is dead." To Harold his words seemed too blunt and cold but he had no idea how to put it more gently. 'Why did they do this?' he raged inside. 'Why send a telegram, why not come down here and explain what had happened.'

"No, he is alive, I know it," she said grabbing the telegram.

"Please dear, don't do this to yourself."

"My darling I'm so very sorry," Clarice said finally but almost choked on her words. She knew she had to remain strong for her daughter but Maria stood in the middle of the breakfast room, with silent tears streaming down her face.

"Would you like a sweet tea?" Harold asked her.

"No, I have work to be getting on with." She dropped the telegram to the floor and put on her hat.

Outside Bernadette and Emma shared a cigarette between them; Doris had told them the news. So it was to both their surprise when they saw Maria leave the house.

"Are you sure you want to work today? Why not rest and get your head together?" Emma tried to put her arm around her sister's shoulder but she moved away.

"I think I would prefer to work."

Bernadette started to cry, "Maria I'm so sorry, very sorry for your loss."

"We both are," Emma ventured.

"I'd rather not talk about it. Emma what needs to be done today?"

"Pulling more potatoes out."

"Fine I will get on with that."

91

Both the girls watched their sister walk away in a cloud of sadness. "I feel so helpless," Bernadette said.

"There is one thing we can do for her and that is do as she has asked. We won't mention Henry and we will get on with the job."

At six o'clock in the evening Emma made her way to the small cottage, just down the path from the school. Jill had rung a few days back and wanted to have a meeting on Richard's progress with the history of the school.

Mr Granger was there at the door, a huge smile on his face. "I have found some wonderful, local newspaper articles on you and your family." Emma smiled but inside her stomach was churning. She walked into the small dining room; the table was covered with old newspapers. "I know of this little old shop in the village, selling antiques and old local news. When I told the owner about you, he said you appeared in a lot of these newspapers."

"Yes, I did lots of interviews for the local press."

"What happened in 1944?"

"What do you mean?"

"It says here that you left the family estate to go to Kent. Why did you do that?"

Emma felt dizzy, but gave an answer, albeit the one her mother had told to tell to say many, many years ago. "I was so well trained, I was asked to become a forewoman."

"Fascinating, tell me a bit about that."

"Much like what I was doing at home, I helped to train the girls to the job they were allocated and made sure they were happy, check that the farmer was happy with their work, make sure their time sheets were correct and that they got paid, that sort of thing."

"Odd, if that is what you were doing at home why did you move?" He smiled smugly at her; he knew something didn't add up, he just could not work out what.

"I can't remember the exact reason."

"Got into trouble did you?" he laughed.

"How do you mean?"

"With one of the stable boys?" he dark eyes glinted with humour.

Emma glared at Jill, who was glaring with embarrassment at Richard. "I doubt anything like that went on," she said with shock.

"No big love affairs then?" he continued.

"I thought you wanted to write about the house, not about me."

"I'm just curious," he said sweetly. "So if we could go back right to the start of your family, when they first built this house, do you have any documents or paintings, that sort of thing."

"Yes I have a few things of interest."

"While you and Richard go through that I will check on dinner."

As she left Richard turned on Emma, "What really went on? Why did you leave? The guy in the village said there was a lot of village gossip about your disappearance. It happened overnight he said."

"You shouldn't listen to gossip Mr Granger."

"Neither should you," he angrily whispered back.

"If you are referring to Matilda, then yes I know of your affair, with a pupil, and I cannot condone such, irresponsible and downright appalling behaviour. You have abused your position of trust and put your wife's job at risk. If you wish for me to keep my silence, you must never see Matilda again, she is just a girl."

"Yes, a girl with a wild imagination. I was kind to her that's all."

"I have seen her enter this house and if it continues I will have no choice but to tell Jill of your infidelity."

"I never touched her, do you really want to put Jill through the delusions of a mentally unstable girl?"

"I don't know what either of them see in you but I promise to keep it to myself if you never see Matilda again."

"I admit nothing but I can promise to stay well away from that crazy girl."

Jill brought in a big dish of cottage pie and then some peas. "How are you getting on, have you found out any secrets yet?" she joked.

When dinner was finished Richard helped her into the taxi, "We are agreed you won't say anything about her lying?"

Emma motioned a cold nod. She left the small cottage with rage in her stomach and an overwhelming wish to expose him for the pond weed he was but couldn't bring herself to humiliate either Matilda or Jill, even though it meant Richard would get away with his unforgivable conduct.

Spring 1941

It had been over a year of hard graft, but Emma was thrilled with what she and her team had achieved. There were beautifully ploughed fields, happy animals and happy workers. It had taken some time to get along with farmer Briggs but even he was impressed by Emma's drive and the other girls' willingness to learn. Not one of them moaned, they all got on with the job with such enthusiasm and pride. As the farm extended and grew so did Emma's army. The government started a drive to get all women to sign up to war work. For many women, the entrapment of war had opened their minds to a new freedom and way of living.

On a rare occasion Emma had the day off she could hear the guns in the background, and orders being shouted as she walked the riverbank and settled under her favourite tree, to read the new book by Agatha Christie, 'Evil under the sun'. She was just getting into it when Major Grey appeared; she had been so enthralled with her book, she hadn't noticed the silence. "You know technically, this is my land," he said in an amused manner. He sat down next to her, "What are you reading?"

"A murder mystery, have you never heard of Agatha Christie?"

"Name rings a bell, but I'm not much of a reader."

"Why aren't you working?" Emma asked curiously.

"I could ask the same question."

"I have a day off; Tuesdays are my full rest days, and Sundays, half. What is your excuse?"

"Lunch break, this is where I come to refuel. Here have half of my sandwich."

"I've just eaten, I won't deprive you. I have never seen you here before?"

"I always come here; it is far away enough from the training ground but not so far away if there was trouble."

For a moment they sat in silence, enjoying the peace of their surroundings. Then the Major started to talk again. "I have a chocolate bar in my pocket." He smiled. "I bet you won't say no to that."

"I am not a child."

"I can see that," he said turning back to his lunch.

She watched him as he ate his sandwich, playing close attention to his hands, which were long and lean but masculine. She could imagine him caressing her with it and then became angry with herself for thinking such thoughts and so became angry with him.

"I am really quite impressed with you, not many girls of your class would roll up their sleeves and get on with such work."

"So you keep saying." He was slightly taken aback by her sharp tone.

"Alright, I'm very sorry." He shrugged, "I suppose I didn't really take you or your sisters seriously."

"Neither did your wife or anyone else for that matter but that doesn't stop me. I don't care what people think, I know what I am capable of."

"You shouldn't pay to much attention to Scarlett." He could see now why she was so peeved. "My wife thinks applying lipstick is hard work." Emma ignored him; she wasn't interested to know anything about his obnoxious wife.

He saw Emma's mouth set in a stern frown. It amused him greatly that she was jealous of his wife, it meant she had feelings for him, he knew he could never act on these feelings so he would not tease her again but his heart did feel a little lighter at the thought of it.

"Do you like it here?" she asked trying to lighten the conversation.

"I do."

"I used to come to this place all the time when…" She trailed off thinking of Nickolas.

"When what?"

"Nothing."

He stared at her, "How is Maria?"

"The truth is I don't know. She won't talk to us; I don't know what to do."

"I'm sure you are helping, even if you don't realise it. Just knowing you're there for her is probably the biggest comfort of all."

"It is not me she wants but Henry. How can life carry on when someone is hurting so much?"

"I know it is a cliché but time does heal." He could see the worry in her eyes and did not want to distress her any longer. "I better get back. I'll leave you in peace with your book." He walked away with a longing to stay to comfort her but his feelings were going beyond a mere fancy, he wanted her. He would have to do his very best to stay away. How, he did not know, when his mind was constantly filled with thoughts of her but he was not a cruel man. Nor did he wish to hurt anyone, least of all Emma, so he walked away and willed himself not to look back.

Emma's disappointment welled within her, she wished she had been nicer to him, asked more questions, taken an interest but she knew if she did that she would be giving into temptation. She put her book down no longer able to concentrate as he turned to look back at her.

2009

Emma took her usual walk into the village, before entering the café she couldn't resist looking out for the little antique shop, it stood next to a Tesco express, appearing completely out of place. She knew now, Richard was telling the truth and if he was to dig too deep he could hinder any chance she might have to getting to know her granddaughter. She needed to put her mind at rest and meet the person who apparently knew a little about her past.

Emma entered expecting to know the person seated behind the desk but the man held no recognition to her.

"Can I help you?" the old man asked.

"Do I know you?" she sounded crazy.

"No, I don't think so," he said looking wholly bewildered.

"My name is Emma Attwood, does that ring any bells?"

"Oh!" he said identifying the name. "Yes your family used to live here, where the school is now."

"Yes, that's right."

There was a silence, she stared at him deeply, watching for a response but there was nothing, he just looked at her awkwardly. He had no idea what she wanted.

"Are you interested in any of the antiques?" he asked desperately.

"Have you lived in this village all your life?" she ignored his question.

"Born and bred. Much like you I guess."

"And you remember me?"

He looked at her quizzically, "I remember your family. Your mother would take tea with my mother." This did not seem odd to Emma. Her mother would often take tea with women from the village indulging in idle chit-chat.

"Who else do you remember? I'm talking back in the war years?"

Now he smiled realising the questions, "Major Grey, that's who you want to know about."

"What about him?" she asked, with her heartbeat quickening, even after all these years.

"He was a good man, wasn't he? He used to put me in the driving seat of his car and let me play in it for hours. I know you two got on very well, because I would overhear mother talking about it. Is that what you wanted to know?"

"I have just moved back to the village and a friend of mine Richard Granger..." Recognition came over the man's face. "...said there was some idle gossip going round. I just wanted to put the record straight for I have family here."

"I never gossip, I just said there was some talk but mother said it was rubbish and scolded anyone in the village who bad mouthed you." Only now did it occur to her, that his mother was obviously someone close to the family.

"Who was your mother?"

"Molly Kurt, she was your cook, I probably shouldn't tell you this but often she would bring home a bit of ham or what ever was left over. You could get a fine if caught wasting food back then so I guess she was doing you a favour."

"Molly was your mother!" Emma stopped to think and then she remembered something, something that at the end she wasn't quite sure if Molly had seen. "You said you overheard your mother talking about me. What did she say?"

"Oh I don't really remember but I know she thought a lot of you. I think sometimes she felt your mother didn't respect you all that much and I suppose she tried to speak up for you. I'm sorry if that hurts you but you did ask."

"It is fine; I thought a lot of Molly." Emma decided not to question anymore, clearly he knew nothing. "I was deeply saddened when her son died."

The old man looked down, "Yes, my older brother. She took it very tough."

"I'm so sorry; I didn't mean to bring back bad memories."

"They weren't all bad, sometimes it's nice to remember."

"And sometimes it's better to forget." Emma walked out of the store; clearly he didn't know anything being just a child. She was sure Molly had once seen them and evidently she never said a word.

Summer 1941

Doris retrieved the post from the postman and brought it through to Mr Attwood, who was eating his breakfast. "Bernie, there is a letter for you here, looks like Derek's writing."

Bernadette quickly opened the letter; she didn't want to show her excitement in front of Maria but she was desperate to hear some news. "He has some leave," she said still reading the note. "In a month's time, he will be back, only a week's leave though." Again she tried to hide her disappointment; at least he was coming home.

"That is good news Bernie, I am pleased for you," said Maria, it was her true feelings but the pain of knowing she would never see Henry again was still hard to deal with. Even after a year since they said goodbye Maria would pray everyday Henry would walk back through the front door.

"Right then I am off." Harold said, which was walking around and checking people's identity cards outside an ammunitions factory. "Bye dear," he said to Clarice.

"The weather has been so nice Scarlett and I thought it might be nice to have a picnic. Would you girls like to join us?"

"That sounds lovely," Bernadette said.

"It's Saturday we have to work," Emma said; she was quite relieved she wouldn't have to spend time with Scarlett.

"That's alright come over in your lunch time. Molly will make up a lovely hamper and we will have a blissful summer's day."

"Where are you having this picnic?"

"I think by the river, near that big old oak tree." Emma felt her stomach churn, she didn't want Scarlett to be at her special place but she conceded and mentally scolded herself for being so childish.

"Alright see you about one, by the river."

Out in the fields Emma kept herself happy by yelling out songs with the other girls while feeding the lambs. Their favourite song was Gracie Fields – Walter. Tom would watch them with a disapproving eye but even he was laughing at the lambs trying to bleat in tune with them.

Come lunchtime, the three sisters made their way over to their mother. Clarice had the full picnic kit out on the grass and poor Doris to wait on them all. Scarlett and Clarice sat elegantly in their chairs, as they watched Bernadette, Maria and Emma fall to the ground, careless of the dry dust rising and clinging to their clothes as they already looked absolutely filthy.

"Will you three ever be clean again?"

"Most unlikely," Emma grinned.

Two fair haired little girls came running out; they had been behind the tree, then followed Arthur and then finally Elizabeth.

"It was Scarlett's idea to bring the children along."

"What a wonderful idea that was," Bernadette said, while scooping up a rather reluctant Arthur. "Go on then run along."

They watched the kids run away; they were playing some sort of war game, trying to defeat the Nazis. Poor Elizabeth could only waddle after them but Maria stopped her.

"You are too young to be playing, come have some food with Mummy," Maria told her before she started to cry.

"Oh those kids, look how close they are to the river." Scarlett could see Arthur dipping his hand in the fast stream. "Kids stay away from the river!"

On hearing her they withdrew and sat on the bank. Scarlett returned to her seat. "Emma, I hear your friend Joe is now fighting away. You must miss him. I remember my first love, it will get easier."

Emma wasn't sure if Scarlett was doing it on purpose but it seemed to her that she was purposely trying to get up her nose.

"It wasn't Joe who Emma liked!" Clarice's horrified voice echoed around them all. "It was a young lad called Nickolas, very wealthy and respectable." Clarice raised her eyebrows in triumph. "But he is now fighting like everyone else."

Emma ignored her mother and spoke to Scarlett. "Joe and I are just friends and yes I do miss him."

Scarlett's attention was away from Emma. Her normally perfect face was crumpled in panic. "Where's Harriet?" she shouted over to the children. Arthur and Louise had their backs to Harriet and when they had turned around she was no longer standing behind them. "Harriet?" Arthur yelled.

"Oh God, she is in the river, she's in the river!" Scarlett shouted in distress. "I can't swim!" Despite making this statement, Scarlett threw off her jacket and ran for the river; she was going to attempt it to save her little girl.

Instinctively Emma dived into the river; she could just make out blonde curls falling beneath the water. She held her breath and swam along the bottom of the riverbed. Mud was clouding her view and stinging her eyes but she kept swimming forward, groping anything she could touch. She came up for breath and quickly divided back in, as her head ducked under the water, she felt a hard kick to the stomach, it winded her. Still she pursued it and managed to grab her by the arm and pulled her to the surface.

Harriet was heaving but at least she was breathing, unlike Emma who was still in pain from the kick. Scarlett quickly grabbed her daughter out of the water. "You silly thing!" She clung to her, crying with relief.

"Oh Edward thank God you're here," she cried. Edward surveyed the situation in shock; he ran to her and held them both tight.

"It's alright my love, she is alright," he reassured her.

Emma was still struggling to get out of the water, her sister tried to help but Emma was still short of breath.

"Please help Emma out of the river," Clarice asked the Major.

He wanted to stay next to Scarlett but did as he was told. He held out his hand to Emma and pulled her away from the river. Emma could sense his reluctance to touch her, almost as if he had just realised what truly mattered to him.

"How can I thank you?" Scarlett asked, still tears in her eyes and clinging to Harriet. Emma could not speak, her lungs felt clogged with mud. "I'm going to take Harriet to the doctors, Emma would you like to come with us and get a check up."

"No, I'm alright," she said finally getting her breath back.

"Edward will walk you home." He remained stone faced; it was not what he wanted to do so once again Emma declined. "You should be with your daughter."

He looked at her with sad eyes, knowing she sensed what he was feeling and then wrapped his jacket around her as her shirt had turned see-through.

"Emma is right," Clarice said. "I will take Emma back, you take little Harriet to the doctors.

Emma walked away from them all even though she had done this heroic thing, she felt hurt and angry, with him and herself, she could no longer help her feelings for him. She loved him.

The next morning they all saw each other before entering church. Scarlett beamed at Emma, "Thank you again for what you did. You saved my daughter's life. Both Edward and I would like to show our thanks by inviting you to ours. I know how hard you work, so come in your lunchtime. Please say you'll come?"

"Thank you but there is really no need. I did what any other person would do." Emma did not fancy sitting and making light conversation with Scarlett or the Major.

"Emma! Scarlett wants to show her thanks, don't be so rude." Clarice showed her up in front of them all.

"Only if you are sure, I don't want to get in your way." Emma turned back to Scarlett

"You wouldn't be honestly," Scarlett reassured her. "When do you take your lunch break? Edward's is usually around one o'clock, is that alright for you?"

Emma saw her excuse, "Oh I'm ever so sorry but we are in the middle of the harvest, we have a rota at what time the girls are allowed to take their lunch and I'm the last today. So I won't be able to get away until about two."

"That's alright but it means just the two of us. We can get to know each other better." Emma managed to smile but inside she felt miserable.

Later that afternoon, Emma knocked on the door to Major and Mrs Grey's cottage. Scarlett opened it with an over enthusiastic smile. Evidently she felt just as uncomfortable as Emma. "Oh you're wearing your work clothes, how lovely." Emma had dry dirt on her hands and bits of corn sticking out of her jumper. Scarlett, who had changed from her church clothes into a lovely floral summer dress, now blocked Emma's entry into the house. "If you go through that gate it will lead into the garden. It is such a lovely day, we can eat outside."

Emma did as she was told, instantly she noticed the garden was filled with vegetables. "Who grows these?" Emma asked Scarlett in surprise.

"Edward. I think you inspired him." She laughed as she put down the tray of tea things and sandwiches. "Please dig in, you must be hungry."

Emma nodded her thanks but any attempt at composure was soon lost for she was starving. Scarlett continued talking, "Tell me, about this Nikolas then, your mother said he is a lovely young man."

"He is but I don't like to talk about it."

"I'm sorry I didn't mean to pry. We haven't always got along have we? But let us start afresh. I admit I did misjudge you and I do sincerely apologize."

"I guess we are two very different people but really there is no need to apologize."

"Oh, well have you heard from that boy, what was his name?" She thought back in her memory. "Oh yes Joe, wasn't it?"

"I haven't heard from him."

"Shame, I suppose he liked that Laura a bit more, I saw them at the dance, hands all over each other. I didn't know where to look!" Scarlett laughed nervously but Emma made no reply. She shuffled in her chair, "Still young love I suppose." Emma merely nodded. "Do you think you will get back together again with Nikolas, if... mmmm." Scarlett trailed off she felt bad saying, if he doesn't die. She didn't even want to bring up the subject again but Emma wasn't making any effort at conversation, she was just stuffing her face.

"I think we will be just friends."

"Oh good, good. Yes keep it friendly. Always best... What about after the war, any plans of what you might do?"

"Not yet."

"I suppose you will get married. A pretty girl like you, you will have them queuing up."

"I hope to continue working or I will get a new job."

"A job? But your family has all this wealth, you don't need a job and you could have any man you choose. Why would you want to work?"

"I like earning my own money and because I have my self-respect. Working on the land has proven to me that I can do anything and I do not have to rely on a man to feed and clothe me. I am quite capable of doing that myself." Scarlett looked away; she knew Emma's stinging remark was aimed at her.

"When you become a wife and mother you will not have time for such modern thoughts. It is a full-time job caring for your loved ones."

"I am sure you are right but I like the thought of contributing, to do something worthwhile with my life."

"If that is how you see things, Emma." Scarlett sat cold never had she felt so small and insignificant. Emma aroused all those feelings in herself that she hated; jealousy and worthlessness. It wasn't normal for her to feel like it but every time she was around Emma, her envy would get the better of her. In her mind Emma had everything in life and everything Scarlett aspired to be but still it wasn't good enough, she couldn't just be grateful for the privileged upbringing God had given her.

Emma knew she had been hurtful and tried to make amends. "How is Harriet?"

"Much better thank you. They are both with school friends, today."

After a few more minutes Scarlett asked about her brothers. "What about your brothers, any news on them?" Scarlett held a secret hope, that when Louise, her eldest daughter, got older she could marry one of them.

"They both seemed to be enjoying flying but we don't hear from them all that much. I guess they are always busy."

All conversation now came to a halt, both looked around, trying to find some inspiration for something to say, but they did not have anything in common.

"I better return to the work," Emma had had enough, so decided to make her exit. "Thank you for lunch, it was very nice."

"You are welcome, I hope you enjoyed it, don't work yourself too hard," Scarlett said with a depth of sarcasm.

When Edward came home, Scarlett had everything ready for him. The food was on the table and the children quietly doing their homework. "This looks nice, my darling. Did you have a good afternoon with Emma?" He tried to make his enquiry seem light.

"She is an odd girl, nothing like her mother. She was very cold and unfeeling."

"Was she impolite?"

"No, just… petulant."

"She probably was tired, what with working on the farm all day."

"No it wasn't that, I know what it is," Scarlett said in a low voice.

"What?" His heartbeat raced with nerves.

"I'm not her equal. She was born into this wonderful lifestyle, while I just try to emulate it. She looks down her nose at me and I think she hates me because I get on so well with her mother; it's more like I am Clarice's daughter than she is. She made me feel very small today."

"Scarlett, let's not forget what she did for us."

"I've said thank you and I have tried to be friendly but she treats me as an inferior person."

"Look at everything you have around, you have created our happy home. There is nothing inferior about you," Edward said calmly, but inside he was fuming. He had an important job to do. He did not have time to hear about some silly feud going on between them. Inside he berated Emma for not making life easy and accepting Scarlett's friendship. "I am going out for a walk to clear my head." He often took a walk after dinner; it helped him to control his anger. Tonight, however, the more he walked the angrier he got. He wished he was fighting, away from all the pointless rubbish that was going on round him. How he longed to be in the action and with the men. It wasn't that he liked war so much but that, he didn't want anyone thinking he was a coward avoiding his duty. The years he spent serving had hardened him, he rarely showed any sign of emotion and any affection given, never touched him. So why was he losing his cool over Emma? Why was this girl getting to him? Over in his mind he saw her reappearing from the river as he helped her out. Without realising it he made his way to the same place and sat beneath the tree.

"Don't turn around; I don't think I could contain my anger right now." Emma sat ahead of him, her legs dangling in the gushing water.

"Then leave, this is my father's land."

"My wife is right about you, you are a spoilt little brat. You can't get what you what, so you have taken it out on someone else."

"And what do you assume that I want?" She turned to him, her cheeks ablaze, her eyes defiant.

"Don't play your pathetic little games with me!"

"I suppose you expect that more from your pathetic little wife!" A heated, angry pause of silence took place, as the two of them glared at one another.

"What do you want from me Emma? I can't change the fact I am married. I can't change how life has worked out. Trust me if I had my way I wouldn't even be here, I would never have met you and I wouldn't have to constantly fight my feelings for you." He breathed a deep breath, "It can never be."

"Then stay away from me, I never want to see you or any of your family. Go back home Edward, go and be miserable, deny what your heart is craving."

"We have to see one another otherwise people will be suspicious."

"Just leave me alone."

"Why can't we just be friends, Scarlett wants to be, so do I. It's just a crush, it will pass."

"Don't patronise me. You keep passing the blame on to me but shouldn't you be with your family, rather than having an argument with me?"

"Have it your way. When you have decided to grow up, I will be happy to be your friend again."

"I have no intention of being your anything!" she screamed scornfully.

Maria greeted a weary looking Derek, it was decided she would tell him in person and not write it in a letter. Bernadette had complied with her sister's wishes and now Maria told him the sad news of her husband's death. "Maria please accept my deepest sympathies," he said.

"Please accept mine, Henry thought the world of you and I know the feeling was mutual." Bernadette stood at her husband's side and held his hand. He tried to control his emotions in front of Maria but once she had left, he broke down into his wife's arms.

"A part of me knew but still this is a big shock. I really did hope that..." His voice started to crack; they were more like brothers than friends.

"I know darling." She stroked the back of his neck. Her own tears falling, she so desperately wanted to cling to him, to not let him go. To berate the world for making such poor choices and getting millions of innocent people involved.

Saturday afternoon and Jill came breezing through Emma's front door. "Thank you for inviting me round. What a lovely home you have!"

"Thank you, go through to the conservatory." Jill walked in and found the table laden with tea and cakes. An old photo album sat next to the tea pot. "I wanted to show you these pictures. I don't know if any will be of interest but one shows the garden before and during the war, which I think is very interesting to the history of the house. I also have one on the family." Jill looked at the photographs with real curiosity.

"These are excellent. May I take these and photocopy them. They will be perfect to put into the booklet."

"Yes of course but please take care of them."

"I promise. I will put them in a plastic folder so they will not get damaged. Richard has done a lot of the writing on the house with all the information you have given him."

"I'm glad to be of some help."

"What I will do is I will make up a prototype of the booklet tomorrow and then leave the photos and the first copy of it on the coffee table in the living room, so you can collect it Monday. Richard should be in but if not here is a spare key to the house just let yourself in. I can't wait to get your opinion on it."

Jill continued to look through Emma's photo album and had a wonderful afternoon chatting with her.

Monday morning and Emma hoped Richard would not be in. After knocking three times and waiting for several minutes Emma put the key into the lock.

She saw the booklet and photos on the coffee table and then saw Matilda's school bag next to the chair. Within moments the pair appeared unaware of Emma's presence.

"I did knock but no one answered."

"What the hell are you doing here?" Richard's blood was boiling, he had been caught out.

"Your wife wanted me to see what you had been up to. Now I have seen it, now I will leave."

"You aren't going to tell her are you?" Richard panicked.

"I told you to stay away Matilda and you promised. What choice have I got?"

"Please Miss Attwood, don't say anything," Matilda pleaded. "It is entirely my fault. Please I don't want to get into trouble."

"Go back to school and stay there." With that Emma left. Jill would have to be informed but it needed to be done discreetly, so Jill could handle it in her own way without the authorities finding out. If Emma were to tell her though why would she believe her, Richard would probably just talk his way out of it. It had to come from Matilda and it had to be soon.

Autumn 1941

Clarice and her daughters were all in the main living room, knitting for the war effort. Bernadette's husband had returned to the army and Jack and William had been in regular contact. Harold was still busy with his home guard duty, as they were calling it now. The war was well and truly in full swing and showed no signs of letting up.

Life now seemed still to Emma, boredom followed her around. She had seen very little of Major Grey since that summer night. Her life was centred around work, the soldiers were not there long enough to really know anything about them and the radio and newspapers were always full of doom. Rationing was becoming ever more stringent and depressing, meat, fats, milk, cheese, eggs and sugar had almost disappeared. Molly was inventive and resourceful but still the food seemed insipid and Emma detested the horrible pale pink blancmange shaped into unidentifiable animals. Life for Emma didn't seem that much different from the food, bland.

"Mother I am going for a walk," she said quite decidedly.

"It's very windy outside; I think you should stay indoors."

"I'll be fine. I need to get some air." Emma threw over a huge woollen coat and hugged it around her.

Outside she could hear the usual sounds of shouting and shooting. It was like a war was going on outside her front door. She made her way to her favourite spot, wondering if Edward would appear. It seemed unlikely. She looked over to the woodland; she could just make out flashes of soldiers running in between the trees. Then all of a sudden things went quiet, nothing on the landscape moved, she knew what this meant and her heart now thumped like crazy. She waited in the desperate hope he might appear. It was a while but then she heard his voice. "You must be freezing?" She was shivering but not through cold. He sat next to her and grabbed one of her hands. "You are freezing. Here have some of my tea." This was a very generous offer, a few weeks after the fall of Dunkirk tea was rationed. Despite the cold of her hands she could still feel the heat of his long past after he let go.

"I needed some air," Emma said, trying to draw attention away from her nervousness.

"How are things on the farm?"

"I have trained my girls well, everything runs like clockwork."

"I wish I could say the same thing about my men," he said.

They sat in silence for a while and watched the multicoloured leaves blow around the landscape.

"I'm sorry for what I said," Emma managed to say, although it hurt her pride and she didn't really mean it.

"Forget it, it's in the past."

"I like coming here, I used to meet a friend here. We were engaged and I loved him very much."

"What happened?"

"He wanted to fight and didn't want me to be pining away. I have no idea where he is or if he is even alive."

"You let him go though."

"I had no choice. What I wanted to say and I know I am making excuses for my immature behaviour is that I put you in a very difficult position because someone else hurt my feelings and I am sorry."

"He was a fool to let you go." Their eyes connected and again there was that thump, which if she wasn't sitting down, would knock her down. She wanted to lean into him and kiss him. To feel what it would be like to kiss such a man, but she turned away. Common sense got the better of her. For a moment though, she thought that maybe she saw disappointment in his face. He turned his head away, breaking away from the intensity of the moment. "I'm seeing your father today," he stated looking at the river. "I need some help, filling in the forms. It's all got rather on top of me. I thought maybe he could suggest someone. If not I will have to go to the war office and they are quite strict, in case the Nazis discover one of our training centres, so it will take quite a while for someone to get here."

"I'll do it," she said before she could really think about what she was saying.

"You have too much work on as it is."

"Tuesday I don't, I'm sure I could cope."

"We could try it for a month or so, but if it gets too much you must tell me."

112

"I will."

He got up to depart and then said, "We will always be friends, remember that, Emma," he stressed to her.

She watched him walk away from her, how heroic he looked in his uniform. He turned back to say, "Don't stay out here too long, you might catch a chill."

Edward made his way back to his office, which was like an air raid shelter, with a window. All the papers were neatly stacked and ready to be sent off, for the war records. 'Why did I do that?' he thought over and over again. He didn't need any help, he just wanted to see her. Guilt flowed though him, she had one day off and now he had taken it away from her. The last few weeks were agonizing not being able to see her and he knew being close to her all day was not going to help matters but try as he might to fight his feelings, he loved her.

"Ah, Miss Attwood," Emma instantly recognized the voice of Mrs Granger travelling down the phone line. "I wonder if you could do me a favour and speak to Matilda Richardson, she told me she would like to leave the school. The thing is she's always been happy here and I know for a fact she doesn't like her aunt. I have tried my hardest to reason with her but she won't listen to me. Would you have a word with her? Maybe you could come to the school, her mood has seemed so sporadic lately. I have run out of ideas to find out what is going on."

"What about her father, won't he look after her?"

"They are not close, I know he keeps in contact but he is not in the country long enough to keep an eye on her. I want her to finish her A-levels and to go on to university but she keeps wanting to hit the self-destruct button. I know she has had it tough but she can't keep using her mother as an excuse to go off the rails."

"Does she have any contact with her?"

"No, none at all, her mother was in her forties when she had her and after ten years, she just could not cope. So she walked out. I know Matilda blames herself but I really think she has to let this go now. I am so very worried about her. Please will you help me? She has refused to speak to me and the school nurse. I don't know what else to do."

"I have Matilda's mobile number I will ring her later this evening."

"Thank you Miss Attwood, I wouldn't ask normally but you are the only one she will listen to. Anyway how have you been? Did you pick up the booklet? What do you think? Has Richard done a good job?"

"Yes I did and I have read through it. I think he has done a good job."

"I am so pleased. I think working on your family history has made him think about our family future." Jill lowered her voice slightly. "We have decided to start a family."

"Oh, really?" said Emma completely shocked. "Was this your idea?"

"No," said Jill; surprised Emma didn't just wish her the best of luck. "No it was his idea, straight out of the blue but I think it was seeing your family tree, gets you thinking doesn't it? Plus I've always wanted children."

Emma could have screamed at herself, she could sense Jill's joy and now she was totally trapped. She ended the phone call abruptly assuring Jill. "I will speak to Matilda tonight."

Matilda sat in Miss Attwood's conservatory looking out across the garden, she kept telling herself she had made up her mind, she was leaving Oakwood. "Matilda? May I be frank with you?" said Emma.

"I'd rather you be Bob," she smiled sarcastically.

"Leaving school is going to make matters worse." Emma had taken the seat besides her.

"No, no it will sort everything out."

"Where will you go?"

"College, I will have to stay at my aunt's but it's for the best."

"Well, I don't think it is. You're letting that man rule your life, if you leave his guilt will melt away and then he could take advantage of another pupil. Could you really have that on your conscience?"

"My conscience is damaged enough, he didn't pursue me. I had the affair with a married man. You have no idea of the guilt I feel whenever I see Mrs Granger and worse still is I can't control my emotions. What if I say or do something that could destroy her world. I don't think I ever really loved him. I'm just addicted to the excitement and maybe if I go, then everything will go back to how it was before."

"You can never go back, you must accept the past and move on. Running away will not solve anything."

"What are you saying?" she whispered very quietly.

"You must tell the truth. Before another life comes into this world and has to be brought up through a broken family. One mistake could lead to years of ramifications. I believe Richard Granger is capable of doing this again and again. You must tell Mrs Granger what he has done, because next time it may not just be her husband she'd be losing but her job."

"I can't do that, I'll be expelled or something. What if the whole school finds out I will be hated," she said in horror.

"Jill will want to keep her job, it's her life. I will do my best to protect you but you must confront what you have done, it's the only way of moving on."

"Can I have time to think about this?"

"You don't have time, I didn't want to tell you this but they are trying for a baby. He thinks he's got away with it, but a baby is just a sticking plaster, Jill knows something is wrong, she just doesn't want to admit it because he has finally agreed to something she wants desperately."

"Why should I be the one to destroy that dream? I'm not going to say anything, so please, please I beg you just let it go. You have no idea what you are dealing with."

"I know exactly what it is like to be your position." Tears formed in her eyes now, it was time for her to confront her own past.

Winter 1941

Emma saw for the first time what happened on the other side of the estate. Hiding in between the trees and foliage sat many large shelters. Each one set up for different purposes. Some were for the new recruits, others were for medical, detail taking and uniform fitment. Beyond the woods were the training grounds, an assault course, deep trenches and target practice. It was a whole world away from her little farm.

At first there really wasn't a lot to be done, so she would sit and watch the training. It wasn't just learning how to use weapons like Emma first thought. It was also learning how to surprise the enemy, come up from behind and tripping them, learning to fight in combat without weapons. Fitness test, tests of endurance, how to operate and aim cannons.

Today it was a new set of recruits, Emma was rushed off her feet but she was just one person in a long line of things that needed attention. When she first saw the men that would be fighting for the country, she couldn't quite believe how they could start off as individual men and end up being a group. No one stood out when they left for battle, their identity seemed lost.

As each solider told Emma their name, address and next of kin, she could tell by their facial expressions how they felt; some were excited, ready for anything, others were quiet, almost as if they were psyching themselves up, others looked petrified, heading into the unknown. Each one had an accent, a story, a sweetheart. She tried to imagine what it must be like to go to war but her small mind could not see it, could never begin to feel it. All this time she had been dancing and laughing with these heroes and she had treated them as if they were normal men, doing normal things. When she would look at a solider now, she would no longer think of them as boys in smart uniforms but men, who were brave and who had family, who deserved the country's respect. Two weeks of training didn't seem enough to let them go into the light of real combat.

All day she watched and wondered. When the day was done and all was quiet again Emma asked Edward, he spoke of wanting to be out there fighting but she could not think why. "What is it like, fighting?" The question shocked him a little, never in his life had he talked about the atmosphere of war. He felt a slight resentment at her for being so curious. Most people had the common sense to leave well alone but he could see that the day had been hard on her. She had been protected all her life from bad things and now she wondered how wrong her image of the world was.

"It is war you don't go there to like it. You see men die, men you like, men you hate. You're isolated, despite the people around you. Deafening noise, of guns, bombs, men screaming. If you are still standing, you have to keep going until you're not. When the battle is over, everything goes eerily quiet, as each side nurses their wounded. No one really talks, just wishes to be out of there, hoping and praying that soon all of it will be a past memory, but it isn't, it's with you for the rest of your life. That's why I hate talking about, it focuses it once again, even the smell never leaves your nostrils, that smell of death. You breathe it in and it feels it destroying what little life you have left in you."

Emma was silent thinking about her brothers going through such hell. Edward continued. "Our boys have to be prepared, not just in fighting but in the psychology of war. Nerves can go at any moment." Edward could feel himself being dragged back into that time, looking out at the mock trenches he could see, so vividly, the horror of each day. His worst memory was a good friend, a comrade talking to him, trying to give him hope because so many lay dead and rotting around him. His speech didn't help but he knew that he was just as frightened as Edward was. With a slap on Edward's back, he went over the top, something hit him, a grenade most likely, he watched his friend be blown apart, right in front of his eyes. He started to shake all over, the intensity of never knowing when it might be you and the shock of how quick your life is taken, without warning. You could vanish in an instant.

Emma stood behind him, watching his body visibly tremble. She put her hand on his shoulder to comfort him. He turned to face her; her blue eyes looked into his with such concern. "I should never have asked, I'm sorry."

"Technology might be a bit better now, but men will die and other men will have to watch. Nothing will ever change that and no one will understand how shocking that can be." She was standing very close to him but he pulled away. "I was wrong to ask you to help here, it's too much for you."

"I want to do my bit, these men are sacrificing so much. I want to at least be brave enough to face them, because they aren't just fighting for their country, but everyone who lives in it."

"You may not know war, but you know hardship, you know strength and bravery, you also know sacrifice. Everything that you can possibly do, you have done. No one can ask more of you." She kissed him, it was slow. His lips lingered on hers, a sigh of satisfaction flowed through him. "You should go."

He knew what he had said but still his grip would not lighten from her waist. He wanted to cry for his weakness but his hands continued to undress her. He tried to find the words of love, but there was so much of the soldier in him, he could only say it through action.

Emma woke up and reality hit her of the night before. Every moment was precious to her and she didn't regret it but she did feel remorse.

Her sister waited downstairs, "Emma!" called Maria. "Come on!" Maria now put everything she had into the farm. It helped her deal with her grief; she could see other young girls desperate to hear from husbands and sweethearts. Some suffering, like her. Knowing their pain and wanting to help, in any small way. She wrote to the Nation Union of Agriculture to improve wages but did not inform her father. These women did not get enough money or respect for the amount of work they were doing, without them England would starve.

"Emma!" she yelled again.

"I'm here." Emma strolled downstairs to meet a rather annoyed Maria.

"And where is Bernadette?" she asked irritated. "Every morning she has been late or too ill to work. It doesn't look good on us!"

Emma held her breath, as Bernadette walked into the hall, she had heard everything. "I'm trying my hardest!"

"Clearly it is not good enough!"

"Stop this!" yelled Emma, "Bernie are you alright you look very pale?"

"She is lazy," Maria said spitefully.

"I'm pregnant actually!" After the first flutters of rage, Bernadette threw her hand to her mouth. She had only told her parents and begged them to keep it to themselves. She didn't want to upset Maria, they had always been so close but after the death of Henry, Maria rarely spoke of anything other than work. Bernadette had no idea how she would take her news.

To Maria the news was like a physical blow, not because she was jealous or unhappy for her sister but because it reminded her, she would not be having any more children with Henry. It was just her and Elizabeth.

"How many months are you gone?" Maria asked.

"Seven."

"You idiot! Why did you carry on working? You could have lost the child!"

"I didn't want to hurt you!"

"Stop treating me like a piece of glass! I won't break."

"This isn't solving anything, Bernie I think you should go back to bed. Maria, can you check that the first chores are done?"

Maria did not answer, she left the house, "I could have handled that better," Bernadette said.

"How have you managed to cover it all this time?" Emma had noticed a little bit of weight gain but nothing to cause suspicion. They had all bulked up with muscle.

Bernadette lifted up her jumper, "A corset. There are loads in the attic."

"Come on I will help you up to bed and don't wear that thing any more. You need to take care of yourself."

"What about Maria?"

"She just needs time, she doesn't mean to take it out on you, it's just you are the closest to her. Things will work out, trust me."

In the afternoon she met up with Edward. "It's too cold!" Emma stated, while trying to walk through the snow.

"Come here then and let me warm you." She fell into his arms and snuggled her face into his chest, as he wrapped his great coat around them both. "I want to move somewhere hot, after the war," she said.

"That does sound nice."

"We could be together then."

"Emma last night should never of happened. You know how much I feel for you but I have a wife. I made my choice many years ago," Edward explained.

"I love you though."

"I love you too. I have tried everything to shut off my emotions but I do love you."

"But we can't carry on like this." Emma understood his predicament.

"I don't want you keeping a secret or lying for me. What do you want to do?"

"I want to be with you." She smiled at him. "It is not ideal but we can remain discreet and no one will know about us. We don't want to hurt anyone, so this I am sure is for the best."

"This is agonizing, I just want to be with you."

"We will be I promise you." She kissed him before he could think of another problem. "I can't stay too long I have to get back to work, we are a girl short thanks to Bernadette not being able to work."

"Good I'm glad she has finally told you, she was pregnant."

"How did you know?" Emma asked, stunned.

"Scarlett told me," he said. Emma hated to hear him speak her name but what she hated more was that, her mother had confided in her.

"Like I said, I better go."

2009

Richard had asked to meet Emma at a small tea room in the village. She had agreed reluctantly, he had sounded desperate, so Emma gave in. Straight away, she sensed his nervousness, "I know I have made a big mistake and I am sorry. Jill never has to find out about this, why do you want to hurt her?"

"I was willing to let it go, until Jill informed me that you two are trying for a baby."

"So, what business is that of yours?"

"The marriage must be in serious trouble if you're turning to family life to keep your marriage together."

"Jill wants a child; I'm giving her what she wants. That is what makes a happy marriage. You wouldn't know."

"If she gets pregnant, will you be looking after her? Or abusing another pupil?"

"I married the woman, doesn't that show my commitment?"

"No not when you're lying and cheating and humiliating her behind her back."

"I know you're an old spinster with nothing better to do than to interfere. But if you make Matilda tell Jill, I will inform her you knew everything for months and never said a word."

Emma fell silent, "You really are a nasty little man."

"I do not want to lose my marriage. Everyone has an indiscretion once in their life and that's all it was. Matilda is a little tart who threw herself at me. Why does Jill have to suffer because of her?"

"I may lose my friendship with Jill over this but it will be worth it just so she can get rid of you."

"I doubt she will, she will fight for me, only a few nights with a cold shoulder. We will soon make up."

Emma called his bluff, "Good let's put it to the test then."

"Just stop it." It was a rather pitiful plea. "Do you know what this could do to my reputation?"

"I cannot believe you are still thinking of yourself. Not only will you devastate your wife but she stands to lose everything. Including her job, something she has worked so hard to achieve. Still you sit here not thinking of her, but of yourself. Worried you might get caught and people thinking ill of you. You will no longer be the respectable ex-teacher, with a love of antiques but the sleazy letch who seduced and had sex with a pupil, who is only just considered an adult. You gave no thought to Matilda, you knew she was damaged goods and still you took advantage. Do you have no shame?"

"Clearly not." Her words had got to him. "I have had enough of you. Stay out of my way and keep your mouth shut, otherwise you might learn that, old ladies tend to fall downstairs." He stood up as he said this making sure he was intimidating and frightening her into silence.

Spring 1942

"Emma!" called Tom, she noticed he had a strange look on his face, you could almost say it was a smile. "Good news! Yesterday I 'ad the man from the ministry of agriculture, looking over the farmland and 'e was happy we are meeting our targets and was very impressed with the running of it. I wanted to say, you 'ave done a brilliant job."

"Thank you sir, that means a lot."

"I 'ad my doubts about you but you 'ave proved me wrong time and time again and so 'ave your girls, so like I said, well done."

"I told you I could do it."

"Alright don't let the praise go to your head. You 'ave to keep up with the same standards!"

"Yes sir!"

'Finally,' Emma thought, 'recognition for all that hard work.' She decided to treat her girls and say a well done to them. She walked over to the girls in the greenhouse, sowing seeds ready for the summer. "Listen up girls; I have just heard we are meeting all our targets for our farm. Your hard work is helping and making a huge difference in keeping this country going, I hope you are all very proud of yourselves. Now tonight, I want us to celebrate our own victory. So I am going to take you all to the pub and buy you all a drink."

A huge cheer went up, and a verse of 'there'll always be an England'. Each group was told, as Emma walked around the farm she noticed what a huge farm it had now become and how many girls were working for her, never did she think she was capable of such work. Then it dawned on her. 'How much are these drinks going to cost me?'

The evening was full of high spirits; the soldiers were already in the pub. It was the first time Emma had been there but they knew her from her work at the training centre. Worryingly for Emma they also knew all the land girls. Clearly this wasn't the first time they had been in here. The weak tasting ale flowed and everyone felt jolly. The gramophone was wound-up and the latest

American music was played. They pushed the tables and chairs to one side and started dancing. Emma was having such a good time she had not noticed Edward standing in the corner. It was only when one of the soldiers threw her up in the air, that she spotted him. After the dance she went over to him, "How long have you been here?!" She had to shout over the loud music and raised voices.

"Ten minutes, your mother sent me!"

"Why?"

"Do you know what time it is?"

"What?"

"Come outside!" They walked out of the pub into the cold night.

"Your mother sent me, it is eleven thirty."

"We still have half an hour then." Emma was about to turn and walk back into the pub, when a thought struck her. "Why were you with mother?"

"Bernadette gave birth to a little girl this evening. She has been taken to the hospital by your father, they are both fine. They just want to make sure."

"I thought she still has another three weeks to go."

"She thought the same thing; I guess her little one didn't want to wait."

"How did you end up being there?"

"Your father called on me at the training ground. He was looking for the doctor but I'm afraid he wasn't there so I went instead, while your father went into the village to find him. It was too late though and Bernadette gave birth before the doctor arrived."

"You delivered Bernie's baby?"

"Yes," He was about to put his arm around her when he saw Sergeant Major Adams descend down the path.

"Sir," he said, looking at Edward. "Miss," then to Emma, before walking into the pub and bellowed from the top of his lungs. "Back to base!"

Edward turned back to Emma, "I think he has got them under control, I'll walk you back home."

When Emma entered the house all was quiet, she made her way to the living room. In the dark she could just make out a figure sitting on the sofa.

"Maria? Are you alright?"

Maria leant forward to reach for the bottle of brandy in front of her. "Did you have fun tonight at the pub?" she asked with such venom.

"Yes, why didn't you come along?" Maria ignored the question; Emma noticed the brandy bottle was half empty. "Is that father's brandy?" Emma continued.

"Yes, he left it out to celebrate."

"So you know about Bernadette, she had a little girl."

"Good for her." Again Emma could hear that spite in her sister's voice.

"Aren't you at least a little bit pleased? You are an Aunt again, and Elizabeth has got another play mate."

"No, how can I ever feel happiness again! Without..."

"Maria you can't take Henry's death out on Bernadette. There are other women in the same boat, who don't have family to support them."

"But I don't want you. I want Henry." She couldn't understand why the pain was still so raw. "I miss him so much." She broke down. "And there is Bernadette, with everything I want. Why? Why me?" she cried with a pain ripping her heart into threads. "Henry is never coming back. Why did he leave me?"

"This isn't helping you," Emma held up the bottle. "You need to grieve. I know another lady who lost her husband and she said to me, that time may not heal the pain but it does heal the shock. Basically you learn to live life without them. I know that is hard to accept now but one day you will be living life again." Maria didn't say anything; she let her sister hold her for the first time and cried bitter tears.

Emma held her sister tight, wanting to take away the agonising heartbreak. Henry wasn't coming back and somehow Maria would have to rebuild her life not just for herself but also for Elizabeth.

2009

"I need to see you." Matilda sent a text message to Richard.

"Sure, when do you want me?"

"I want to talk, that is all."

"Yes ok. Jill will be busy tomorrow night; I will find you tomorrow and tell what time to come round."

"Cool, I mean it though. Only talk."

"Wear red underwear."

Summer 1942

Scarlett made her usual appearance on Wednesday morning to gossip with Clarice. "How is poor Maria doing?" she asked with true sympathy.

"I think she is coming to accept it now, but digging in those fields is not going to help her find another husband. If I say that though, she will get angry and say I'm unfeeling. I just want her to be happy and I know that there aren't many men around these days. So she has to look her best. The competition will be fierce."

"You know, Edward has an older brother, Phillip, he owns two toy factories that now produce guns or something, for the war. Anyway he's divorced and rather lonely, maybe it might be nice if him and Maria met. He is a lovely man."

"What a good idea, but we can't make it obvious. It has to happen in a natural way."

"Leave that to me, I will get Edward to invite him to stay for a while, he doesn't live far but he has a bad leg, so we only see him when Edward drives him over. Before the war he had a chauffeur but he gave all that up, he wanted to sacrifice something for the war and petrol was the easiest but now he doesn't get to meet a lot of people."

"Shame, well I think they sound perfect for each other. We will have a get together here and introduce them."

"I don't want to make her angry or upset. I would hate her to think I was interfering."

"No of course not, she will never know, we will be very subtle."

Emma had finished her day out in the searing hot dry fields and was now ready for a cooling bath and getting an early night, when she heard her father. "Emma, come in here." As she went into his office, she noticed a photograph of his home guard army, hanging on the wall in pride of place. Below it stood Major Grey.

"Good evening Emma," Edward said unable to make eye contact with her.

"Good evening sir."

"The Major came to check up on your sister and I got him chatting. I am sorry look at the time. Your wife will have put away dinner by now. Are you hungry? Emma take the Major down to the kitchen, see if cook has any leftover's."

"It's alright sir. I'm glad to hear Bernadette is doing well. I won't trouble you any longer."

"No trouble," Emma quickly said. "I will get you something to eat."

Edward didn't want to seem rude, so he accepted by smiling awkwardly.

As they entered the kitchen, Edward began to talk, "I don't like deceiving your father in his own house."

"But on his land, it's alright?"

"Emma, I'm walking around feeling constantly guilty."

"Then walk away." Her eyes stung with tears. She pretended to busy herself with some food.

"I have been trying to do that ever since we met but the problem is, I love you." She stopped what she was doing to look at him. "Forget about the food, just come here." He wrapped her up in his arms and kissed her lips. "You're so beautiful, meet me tomorrow by the oak tree for lunch."

"Edward I…"

"Yes?" As she tried to tell him her feelings, Molly the cook bashed her way through the kitchen in her apron and house slippers. They both jumped back away from each other.

"Is everything alright, Miss?" Molly asked Emma.

"Major Grey is hungry; I was looking for some food."

"Not to worry, I have some cold chicken in the larder," Molly said as she bustled her way over.

"No, please. Do not bother yourself; I will eat when I get home." He quickly left, after giving Emma a discreet nervous glance.

"I was going to make your mother some Ovaltine, would you like some?" Molly busied herself, moving effortlessly around the kitchen.

"Thank you, I will."

"He's a good looking chap; I bet his wife has a hard time keeping her eye on him." Had she seen something? Was this her way of telling Emma to be careful? "Here you go; you'll have a good night sleep on that," she said as she handed her the cup of Ovaltine. "You need to take better care of yourself, dear."

"I'm alright, honestly."

"I see you in the fields, working so hard, and a girl of your class. I knew it would be the making of you but you are taking on too much."

"I'm happy to work, if only to give you ingredients to make such delicious meals."

"I'm serious; you have taken on too much, why don't you take a little break away, you and Maria. Do you both a world of good. You might meet a dashing young man. Being stuck here in your youth can be no fun. You need to be out there having the time of your life."

"I think Hitler had other plans."

"Yes, if only he had walked away and thought of the pain he would bring to people," Molly said this slowly looking deeply at Emma. "But people rarely think about the consequences of their actions."

"No I guess not, maybe I will have that break away."

"Do you both a world of good."

"I'll think about it." Emma kissed her cook on the forehead. Molly put her arm around her and gave her a quick squeeze.

"You're a good girl. Sweet dreams, Miss."

2009

Matilda made her way to the cottage. It was this time last year, she made her move on Mrs Granger's husband. 'What was I thinking?' she asked herself. She had been stupid and needy, and now she despised herself. The first flush of secrecy and excitement and the knowledge of successfully seducing another woman's husband had now left her with a bitter taste in her mouth. There was never any competition, she was younger, prettier, more exciting. The game had been unfair, the winner had been Richard, she had been used and Mrs Granger betrayed. Tonight was the night, it was going to end. Richard had found her earlier in the day and asked to see him tonight. "Jill will be out at the first year's parent meeting and she won't be back until after twelve."

"I don't think it's a good idea." Matilda had tried to back out but he had begged her.

"Please we need to talk, to sort things out."

Now she was outside his cottage, knocking on his door. He answered with a smile on his face.

"Coming in?" His smile was sly; he knew he looked good in his striped shirt and jeans.

"No let's go out" she said quickly with a pang of lust. She didn't want to enter the house; to be alone with him would be dangerous.

He shrugged, "Fine, I'll grab my car keys."

He drove them to a wine bar; he had taken Matilda there once before, but had never gone with Jill.

Instantly Matilda felt the oppressive atmosphere, low lighting hid faces. She hadn't noticed it the first time, but the place smelt of infidelity and deceit. Matilda now understood how he saw her, as a dirty little secret.

"Here, I bought you an orange Bacardi Breeze." She took a sip. He began to talk to her in his usual condescending manner as if she wasn't mature enough to comprehend the situation. "You know how much I care for you. I'm worried about you, if you tell Jill about our relationship you will ruin your life, it shall be scarred forever. All over one silly little mistake and you don't want that do you?"

"I have no intension of telling anyone."

"Good, I'm glad that old witch didn't get to you."

"Don't speak about her like that."

"Sorry, why don't we go back to my place and we can put this misunderstanding behind us. I will do my very best to make it up to you." There was that sly smile again.

"I have said I won't tell anyone, why risk it all again? Quit while you are winning."

"I like having you in my life and anyway in a few months you will be leaving school. There will be a natural break, so we might as well enjoy the time we have left."

Matilda drained her bottle, "No." She left her seat and headed for the door. The cool breeze relaxed her tense body.

"I really don't understand you, one minute you're all over me like a rash the next as cold as ice. What do you want from me? Why can't we just have fun, that's what you said at the time."

"I made a mistake, I know it was my fault, I threw myself at you." She started to cry, never had she felt so low and cheap. He put his arm around her and kissed her face.

"Get in, I'll drive us back."

The journey back was quiet and during that time Matilda managed to pull herself together again. She knew she wanted to end it.

When they pulled up outside the cottage, Richard got out and then opened Matilda's car door for her.

"You're not coming in, are you?"

"No, it is for the best."

"I haven't treated you all that well and I am sorry. I suppose I was angry with you, for making me so weak." He kissed her tenderly, "I couldn't say no to you, you are... well... you are beautiful. My ego got the better of me," he sighed deeply. "I suppose this is goodbye."

"It's for the best," she repeated with conflicting feelings. He kissed her but a noise like a twig breaking made them both jump. "What was that?"

"I think it was just an animal." It was enough to shake her back to her senses. She finally walked away, it was over between them.

Autumn 1942

The job was now really getting to Emma, early dark mornings and not enough hours to get everything done. Potatoes had to be pulled up from the ground, tomatoes had to be picked, lettuces had to be chopped and apples had to be cropped, along with many other fruits and vegetables. Not to mention the animals to take care of and although her girls worked hard it always seemed to be left to Emma to finish off any outstanding job. It could be dreary at times and today felt like that.

By five o'clock she told the girls to go home, it was unfair to keep them any longer as the nights were so quick to get dark. They all had to get back to the hostel and there were no lights or signposts to help them get back. They would just have to remember which road to take.

In the barn Emma divided the carts full of fruit and vegetables into different boxes, ready for Tom the next day. She had a good view of the house from the barn and had watched her mother make her way to her with an excitable step. "Ah Emma and Maria, I'm glad I found you. Tonight we are having the Grey's over for dinner. I want Maria to help me set everything up."

"Why can't Bernadette help and anyway Molly and Doris always take care of that sort of thing," Emma said.

"Bernadette needs to rest and I am asking Maria, not you." Clarice glared at Emma, she wanted Maria scrubbed and looking her best for when the Major's brother arrived.

"Sorry Mother, we have been pulling vegetables all morning, now we have to get them into the boxes. I can't help you." Maria was deeply suspicious of her mother; she was relieved to have an excuse to turn her down.

"Well don't be late. Look at you both! Covered in mud, I want you both scrubbed, cleaned and ready by six o'clock." Clarice gave her daughters a disdainful look before leaving them.

By seven o'clock it was just the two of them, but neither was working particularly hard. "We have to go back sometime or mother will be fuming," Emma told Maria.

"I know what mother is doing, she is trying to set me up with that man."

"You don't know that, he could be a salesman." Earlier they had seen Major Grey and a man enter the house, he walked with a slight limp. Maria had started to panic and decided not to go home for dinner.

"You know full well what she is up to. That's why she came to see us today. Are you in on this?"

"No, I had no idea. Anyway like I said you don't know who he is yet."

"Why is she doing this to me? What about Henry, what will he be thinking?"

"It might be good for you, like getting back on the horse after you have fallen off."

"I'm a married woman," Maria said defiantly.

"Henry would want you to move on and meet someone else, someone who will make you happy again."

"I will never be happy again."

"You can't wallow in it forever, Maria. Other people suffer a lot worse."

Before Maria could give Emma a good tongue lashing Tom walked in. "You girls should 'ave had been home long ago."

"Mr Briggs! Sorry I was miles away. We're still not finished; I have another cart over there." Maria would work all night to avoid anything her mother had planned.

"Don't worry; I'll take care of that. You get off home."

"Come on otherwise mother will come looking for us." Emma grabbed Maria by the arm and made their way back to the house.

"This is my brother Phillip, Mr Attwood," said Major Grey, "He is the reason I joined up to the army."

"That's right blame me, mother never did forgive me," he joked.

"Good to meet you at last Mr Grey. Do you know I have been on patrol at both your factories? But every time I was billeted there, I was told you were out."

Phillip laughed. "Yes I take too many business lunches and dinners. I have a very efficient secretary, Mrs Smith; she deals with the girls a lot better than I do."

"Always the way, it's like my youngest daughter Emma, she's joined the land army, brilliant she is, simply brilliant. You will meet her and Maria my other daughter soon, they're still working at the moment." Mr Attwood gesticulated towards the living room, "Come and meet my wife and eldest daughter."

"Major Grey, where is your wife?" Clarice chirped up, thrilled her plan was coming together.

"I have been to collect my brother, but she should be here any moment. Phillip, this is Lady Attwood."

"How do you do," Clarice said, looking at Mr Grey approvingly. He was handsome, like his brother but more distinguished.

"Do you not drive then?" asked Harold

"I don't, my knee had a bullet through it during the war and it completely shattered the bone. I can walk, just about but it's too weak to drive. Just as well really, what with the lack of petrol."

"Yes, most annoying, we can't even take the Rolls out anymore! To be honest I think Harold refuses, so not to upset the neighbours."

"We must show our solidarity, Clarice."

"Well it's all very vexing." As she said this Doris walked through the drawing room door followed by Scarlett. She was holding a plate, on it sat a sponge cake.

"Ah, I made this, tell no one or I might be shot!"

"How delightful a cake, powder of real?" Clarice asked.

"Real, I sneaked a couple of eggs when no one was looking. I'm afraid no dried fruit or canned peal. They have stopped production!"

"Abominable!" Clarice shouted.

They had all been talking about an hour and a half when Maria and Emma came in, muddy and sweaty, with their shirts hanging out. "Look how late it is, I told you to be back early tonight. Go upstairs now and get washed and dressed." Clarice turned back to the company and smiled. "There are people under all that mud."

"Before you two disappear have a slice of cake," Scarlett offered, cutting two generous slices. Emma grudgingly thanked her.

"You're all doing your bit," Phillip said to the family. "I bet you're not working in the fields, Scarlett?"

"I do my bit; anyway I have two children to raise."

135

"Hardly a strain." He liked teasing his sister-in-law.

"Why don't you join the Home Guard?" she retaliated.

"I can barely walk, let alone rugby tackle a bunch of Nazis to the ground."

Clarice, upset to be pushed out of the conversation, pushed her way back in. "Tell us about yourself Mr Grey?"

"He's divorced," Scarlett spoke up. "Awful women, quite unsuitable for such a fine chap. Actress – you know what they can be like... flighty."

"That's enough, Scarlett," the Major said, embarrassed for his brother."

"Quite alright, it's all true anyway." Phillip gave an easy smile. His grey hair was beautifully combed, but the colour did not age him, he had no lines on his face. To Clarice he seemed laid back and easy going and clearly quite wealthy. He seemed very suitable for Maria.

Emma and Maria returned looking fresh faced and smelling sweet. "Father we need to talk to you," Maria said, she was going to do her best to ignore the Major's brother.

"No, we can ask any time," begged Emma, but Maria continued.

"We need extra help on the farm, could you ask for a couple more girls?"

Clarice rolled her eyes with despair; she did not want Maria talking about farm work with her father when she should be trying to impress the handsome man. "Maria, Emma, I want you to meet Phillip Grey."

"Nice to meet you," Emma said but Maria merely nodded and turned back to her father. "Can we have two more girls?"

"Yes alright, I will try and talk to the hostel tomorrow." Harold was feeling uncomfortable, he thought the whole scheme was a bad idea. Maria seemed incredibly irritated and poor Mr Grey looked disappointed.

"No we have..."

"Maria enough about work, go and find Doris and ask if Molly is ready to serve," Clarice interrupted. Maria did as she was told and Emma followed her out.

"Maria, how could you, that poor man. It's not his fault mother is so pushy."

"I'm not ready for all of this, it's too soon."

"You're not marrying the man, just be polite to him."

"I don't want to give him any ideas."

"And what makes you think he will like you?" Emma teased.

"Hey!" Maria laughed it was the first time in ages and it felt good.

"Molly, is the food ready?" Emma asked

"We can go through to the dinning room." Maria said walking back in.

In the dinning room Harold and Clarice took their normal places at either end, while Bernadette, Phillip and Maria sat on one side and Scarlett, Major Grey and Emma sat on the other. Scarlett and Clarice continued to chat and gossip. Emma tried not to make eye contact with Edward but every so often he would turn to speak to her and there would be a secret smile between them.

Scarlett leant over her husband to talk to her. She still hadn't forgiven Emma but had decided to be civil. "How are things going with you Emma, I hope my husband isn't working you too hard, what with you also doing the farmer routine?" she giggled.

"I just get on with it, the farmer routine and all, as you put it."

"The young are always so serious," she said to Clarice excusing Emma's sharpness before turning back to her. "I was only teasing you." Emma smiled, inside she was fuming.

"Emma would do far better working full-time for your husband. A much more respectable job, although..." Clarice, who sat at one end of the table, with Harold at the other, leant into Scarlett and quietly said. "I think Emma has developed a little crush on your husband." Edward sat in between Scarlett and Emma, had heard Clarice's teasing remark; he sat rigid listening to his wife's reply.

"Little girls always do," Scarlett said tickled.

"Talking of the farm, I have already asked the hostel and they are full, no more girls available. I think if we want more workers the new land girls will have to stay here," Emma said thinking it would be good to have two more workers who could work late and not have to worry about the girls having to ride home in the dark.

"Here!" Clarice said suddenly alert.

"Here," repeated Emma, "they can share a room. We really need their help."

"Will we have to feed them and clean up after them?"

"Clarice, I'm sure they will look after themselves." Emma's father came to her rescue. Clarice looked unimpressed but her attention moved back to Phillip and Maria, they seemed to be getting on.

Phillip kept helping Maria out with portions of Lamb, while Harold twittered on about the war. "We will soon know what is really going on with this war; one of my boys has got some leave. In a month's time William will be back."

"It is going to be a long war that is for certain. The Japanese are storming through," Phillip said.

"Now the Americans are joining the war, at least we stand a much better chance of pulling it back," Edward said.

"I'm pleased Russia has swapped sides, means my friend Alexis can come out of hiding."

"I do not think Russia had a choice," Phillip concluded.

"Hitler is mad, turning on the Russians like that. Now he has to fight two wars, a loss of money and men. He will never win this war now. History will repeat itself; Napoleon couldn't do it and neither will Hitler," Edward said.

"From what I hear Russia is really suffering, it won't be long before it is in the Nazis hands." Emma had seen the news reels at the pictures.

"Don't underestimate the Russian spirit. They have an inner strength. Look at my friend Alexis, everything he has been through and still he pushes on, a remarkable man."

"Oh do stop talking about war, it is so depressing!" Clarice was getting annoyed with the men; it was ruining Maria and Phillip's conversation.

Phillip asked how Maria was coping with working so hard on the land. He knew of her loss and so wanted to keep the conversation to topics that would not distress her or make her feel uncomfortable.

"I find it quite therapeutic," she smiled. "Takes my mind off other things and even Elizabeth grows her own tomatoes. She only allows one tomato to each person."

"How old is your little girl?"

"She is two and very cute. Do you have any children?"

"No, I always wanted some but…well it never worked out that

way. I am a pretty good uncle, although I don't get to see them all that much now."

"Why's that?"

"Petrol, I gave my driver a different job. I needed to do something to help the war effort," he laughed awkwardly. "Scarlett sometimes brings them over to me, I suppose because she thinks I'm lonely but when I'm feeling up to it I will walk over here, takes me a good three hours but I'm sure the walking does me good."

"And are you lonely?" she asked so quietly it was barely audible.

"On occasions, not tonight though, you have kept me in very good company." He patted her hand and then wished that he hadn't. Although Maria knew he didn't mean any harm, she withdrew her hand quickly. 'He's only trying to make friends,' she told herself.

"Next time you go on a long walk, I would like to come with you." Maria regretted saying this as soon as she had spoken the idea because he looked so happy.

"Really, yes I will do that. I could walk over and stay the night with Scarlett and Edward, and then we could go out for a walk the next day."

"Oh good," she smiled nervously.

"You could show me around the farm, it would be interesting to learn what you do." With this she now smiled comfortable, at least now she knew what they would be talking about and maybe they would be friends.

Both Scarlet and Clarice smiled smugly at each other.

Emma met Edward for lunch at their favourite spot but it didn't look like him. Not the man she knew. "This has to end," he said pacing the ground.

Emma staggered slightly, completely shocked at his charge of heart. "Why?"

"Because I am a married man, I have children. I've been so stupid; I never should have got involved with you." Emma was unable to speak, he had winded her. "I cannot go on betraying people who have put so much trust in me."

"But you said you loved me." Violent tears flowed down her soft cheeks.

139

"What good will come of us continuing? I am supposed to be here doing my duty to my country. Emma, if we continue we are going to get caught. Molly saw us in the kitchen, your mother at the dinner table. It is too risky and I am not just thinking of myself. What about your reputation?"

"You sound like my mother now."

"But you understand where I am coming from."

She clung to him, quietly sobbing with regret, "I understand." She finally managed to let him go and returned back to work as if nothing had happened.

He watched her walk calmly away, with such a pain in his own heart. Someone was going to get hurt if the affair continued and he knew that would be Emma no matter what happened. She was too good to be dragged down by such a scandal if they were caught. Never in his life had he loved anyone like he did her, but it was true what he had said, his main priority was to his family. He needed to let her go.

2009

Linda May stood nervously in front of her mirror, with three other girls putting the finishing touches to their make-up. "So, we really are going to do this?"

"Yes, it's simple," Erica replied. "The school will stay open for hours, thanks to the first years parent meeting."

"We will get caught with so many people about."

"No we won't, everyone will be busy in the hall. If you don't want to go, you don't have to?"

Now Louise spoke up, "Linda you have to go, we are eighteen! We are old enough to do as we wish and no one can stop us."

"You're right," Linda said, she sounded convinced but she wasn't. She glanced at herself in the mirror; it had taken her an hour to get her hair just right. She was going out.

The clock struck ten. "Ready?" asked Louise, the girls nodded their reply. Jo stuck her head around the door to take a quick look down the corridor. "We are clear to go."

They descended down the corridor, down the stairs and out of the side door into a small courtyard. Outside they could hear the rumble of chairs and heavy voices coming from the main school hall. To the right of them stood the Art blocks, they split into single file and crept behind the Art rooms. They were now at the back of the school, all that stood in their way of freedom was a hedge but thankfully there was a gap, made by other pupils from previous years, so they could get in and out of school without being detected.

Finally they were on the pavement of the main road. "Where to now?" asked Erica.

"This was your idea!" replied Louise.

"Look, the bus is pulling up. Let's go into town." Jo pointed out the vehicle.

Each one of them ran across the road and jumped onto the bus. A ten minute drive later and they were in the town ready to party. Straight away they could see two venues buzzing, their bright lights filled the street and the bass of the dance music thumped in their hearts. Casually they made their way over to the queue. "How long do we have to stay outside for?" Linda asked her friends.

141

"I have no idea, oh hold on, we're moving forward."

Another ten minutes later and they had reached the front of the queue; the bouncer looked down on their young faces.

"ID?"

"Yes." Each girl took out their driving licenses.

"Alright go through."

"Stop right there!" All of them cringed, they knew that voice well.

"Mrs Granger."

"I'm too busy to deal with you now, so get in the car and don't say a word to me!" She reached her car and opened it for them all to get in. "I'm so disappointed in you all. When you go back home, you can go to all the night clubs you want but not under my care." She drove into the car park and after parking turned in her seat to talk to them. "I don't want you four walking through the hall, it will give the parents a bad impression about how the school is run. You will have to go the long way round and before you get any ideas, I will be back to check on you all in an hour."

Deflated, the girls walked past the new Maths block and started to trek their way to the entrance to the old school building.

"How did she know we had left?" Linda asked, she felt so ashamed of herself.

"Shh, get down!" Erica whispered loudly.

A car had just turned right, down to where Mrs Granger lived.

"I thought I saw Matilda in that car."

"No, it was too far away," Jo replied in disbelief.

"Let's take a look."

"We have to get back," Linda pressed; she didn't want to get into more trouble.

"Just five minutes."

The four of them crouched down behind a bush and watched Mr Granger open the car door, to their shock Matilda got out.

"I can't make out what they are saying," Louise whispered.

"Shhhh," Erica pleaded. Mr Granger was kissing their friend; they all felt slightly sick with jealousy.

Linda's legs were starting to hurt so her she moved her knees onto the ground to take her weight, breaking a twig as she did so. The girls froze as Mr Granger and Matilda looked their way but soon Matilda walked away and he went indoors.

"What happened there?" wondered Louise.

"We have to get back," Linda said again.

"I can't believe this, Matilda told me she was working late in the library."

They ran back through the courtyard and up the stairs, each one bursting to get into their room. Matilda was in bed reading when they finally had finished fighting off each other.

"Well how was your night?" Matilda gave a small giggle; she knew they were back too early.

"We got caught, what about you, how was your night?" Louise asked with a sly smile.

"Good, I got my work finished."

"Really? And what work was that? Chemistry?" she pushed.

"Right girls!" Mrs Granger walked in without knocking. "I'm so angry; I can barely look at you!"

"Sorry Mrs Granger." The four girls said in unison.

"Sorry isn't good enough, you have let me down. Tomorrow you will meet me in the field at six a.m. You will be running three laps as punishment and your parents will be informed."

The girls merely nodded, "I'm glad to see you didn't take part Matilda." Matilda didn't reply, she felt just as ashamed as the rest.

"How did you know we had left?" Louise was still baffled.

"CCTV, Mrs Stanley saw you in the courtyard, dressed to the nines." Jill couldn't help but laugh, she sat on the end of Matilda's bed. "I know you're all in a rush to grow up, but you will have plenty of time to be adults. Just enjoy being young because when you're my age you develop regrets, things you should of worked harder at, like studies. By the end of this school year you will all be in university and be having all the fun in the world. I hope responsibly, so please, don't wish your lives away."

After Mrs Granger left, Matilda sobbed silently, she had betrayed the only person who had truly ever cared for her.

"William is here!" Emma yelled, and greeted her brother with a big hug.

"William we have missed you." William kissed his mother's tear-stained cheeks.

"Hello all, this place doesn't change much," he said looking around.

"William, where have you been?" Emma asked.

"Egypt, very hot there, spent most of my time in Cairo."

"We have heard good news from the north of Africa," Harold beamed at his son.

"Yes, all rather exciting, few months ago Rommel was chased out and we captured a lot of the German army. Yes it looks like we are now starting to make some headway on this war. We have started to advance into Libya. Now where are all these land girls you're training, Em?"

"You stay away from those girls," Clarice said suddenly alert.

"You're right mother, I am married to a French nurse. I have to be on my best behaviour."

"What!" He fell about laughing, it was true but he wasn't going to force the truth.

"It's good to be home. Where is my new little niece then, and have you heard from Jack?"

Bernadette came down the stairs with Ivy her little girl. "I thought I heard your voice."

"Hello poppet. She looks just like you."

"You say that to every girl and her baby."

"It's easier, that way. And Jack?"

"Fine, we received a letter two days ago."

Maria walked in from the back of the house; she guessed that William had no knowledge of Henry's death.

"Good to see you Maria," he said hugging her.

"Good to see you too. I'm afraid I have some bad news."

"I know mother informed me, I'm ever so sorry." William really could not take another tale of death. When a pilot didn't come back they just accepted it.

It was time to do the threshing and Emma was not looking forward to it. She would need a dozen workers and it would take all day to get all the corn threshed. Both Bernadette and Maria said they were too busy helping mother arrange a dinner party for William. So Emma went and found the girls who would do it. Normally there wasn't a lot to do on the farm at this time and so it was the perfect time to get the threshing done. The big red machine would be bought out and it would chug along making the grain pour out into bags, the straw would come out the other end and dust would gather underneath it. Two girls would have to work the machine itself, the string that held the corn together would have to be cut while another girl would feed it through with a pitch fork, if she let too much go down at once there would be a choking noise before it returned back to its normal rhythm. One girl would stand in the cart among the pile of corn, passing them down. One girl would have to check on the bag as it filled with grain. Another would bind the freshly cut straw. The worse job and the job Emma knew she was going to get today because every one hated it, was cleaning up the dust and short straw that came out underneath the machine. If this was not cleaned away the machine would clog up and stop working. After a few hours of clearing out the dust Emma could feel herself covered in it. She could barely breathe, it sank into her lungs, the cold winter air did nothing to cool her and she was red as a beetroot. Sweat ran down her face, each time she cleared a pile of dust, another one would appear in seconds and it would rise up and choke her. No one ever offered to switch places with her.

When the day ended all the girls had worked very hard, it was difficult and tiring to pull up the corn, cut the bound, pass to the next girl to feed through the drum, every girl had to work to a fast pace, to keep the rhythm of the machine going but it was another important stable of the British diet that people needed to keep going. "Well done girls. Load up the bags of grain on the cart, go and get a horse and store it in the barn. I will drive the tractor back." By the time Emma got home it was past seven. What she hadn't known, was that Clarice had invited the Grey's over to join in William's dinner.

Emma walked into the living room covered in a layer of dust, only sweat lines showed her pink skin underneath. She stood there as the whole company of people stared at her.

"I know this is your house Emma but really you could have made a little bit more of an effort," Scarlett joked.

Clarice laughed, "You look like you have been up a chimney. It's even in your hair, what on earth have you been doing?"

Emma wanted to cry, she was tired, Edward was staring at her and she looked ugly and smelt. In a small voice she told them she would not be down to dinner.

"It is William's night. Go and get washed and come back down," Clarice told her.

Tears welled in her eyes, "Mother, I am tired, I will see William tomorrow."

"Once you are clean, you will feel better," Harold said cheerfully.

Slowly Emma made her way up the stairs to her room; she lay on the bed crying. Ten minutes later the door opened, no knock. The tears had blurred Emma's vision but with a rub of her eyes she saw it was Edward who stood in front of her.

"I should not be here; they think I have gone to the loo."

"Why are you here?" asked Emma scorned.

"I care about you, you know that, even when you look like a chimney sweep," he laughed

"Please just go," Emma began to cry again.

"If that is what you want." He waited for her to answer but she did not move. "What can I do, this is painful for me as well."

"Go away, go back to your perfect pretty wife." He did as she asked, but it hurt, he too felt empty and low without Emma in his life.

After he had left her Emma made her way to the bathroom to wash away the grime and the tears of the day.

Putting on a plain white dress she made her way downstairs, they were in the dinning room waiting for the first course to appear.

"Why have you worn that old thing?" Clarice was on her straight away.

"It's what I feel comfortable in." She desperately wanted to shout at her mother and tell her she would wear what she liked and could not care less what she thought, however, it would probably lead to her being thrown out the house, so she kept her mouth shut.

"I bet you look dashing in your RAF uniform. Do you have lots of stories to tell?" Scarlett asked, giving him an over friendly smile.

"Many, like in the sizzling heat I managed to take out twenty German planes, and I, all alone in the sky."

"What nonsense you talk," she giggled.

"It's true; I'm a hero out there. They wanted to make me a Pharaoh. Fancy being my Queen?" he asked her grinning from ear to ear.

She laughed with glee. "I don't like to be too hot."

"They do not wear many clothes and I would be happy to fan you." His voice was a silky whisper in her ear.

Edward watched his wife with disdain; she was making such a fool of herself. Sometimes he really detested his wife, if only he had some sense to stay away when they first met. If only Emma could be his. He kept having to tell himself he had made the right decision, it was not for Scarlett's sake but for Emma's. He had fallen in love with her and she could do so much better than he.

Emma had watched Scarlett flirt with her brother all night, Edward barely raised an eyebrow. 'How could he stay with that awful woman?' she asked herself but even she could understand his reasons for not wanting to continue an affair, even though it seemed so unjust, that fate had thrown them together only to be broken apart by an undeserving, self-centred woman.

After dinner they all retired to have drinks in the drawing room. Edward took his wife to one side for a private word. "What do you think you are doing?"

"Enjoying myself, is that a crime?"

"Will you stop flirting with the boy; you are old enough to be his mother."

"Rather hypocritical of you."

"What is that supposed to mean?"

"I've seen the way you look at Emma."

"You are talking rubbish and making a fool of yourself and of me," he said in an angry whisper.

"William is giving me some attention, something you have failed to do all our married life." With that he made his excuses and left.

As glad as Emma was to have her brother home for a little time, it hurt tremendously to see Edward so dejected. She still didn't understand why they couldn't have carried on as before, Scarlett showed no thought for his feelings and when she openly flirted with William, it seemed clear to Emma, Scarlett did not love or respect him. She knew her relationship with Edward could not go anywhere but she didn't care. She just wanted to be close to him, even though it would be difficult she decided to keep working for him, if only to see him. However, her work on the farm was still heavy, with the help of two new land girls it would take the burden off and give her the time to work for Edward.

Emma woke up early to drive to the train station taking Bernadette's small Green Austin. She waited as the two girls stepped off the train in their new uniform. "Hello, my name is Emma." Straight away she noticed, neither of them were wearing their oil skinned winter coats. "Why aren't you wearing your coats? You must be freezing."

"We were not sent them, miss."

"Please call me Emma and your names are?"

"Joan."

"Norma."

"Well this way, the car is over there. So are you both from London?" It turned out that they both were and had had no training whatsoever. "Not to worry, just listen to me and we will have you trained up in no time."

They both squeezed in the back of the Austin with their luggage. "I warn you my mother is quite talkative, she'll want to know all about you. Now, Tom Briggs is the farmer but he just walks around making sure we are doing everything right. He can be a bit difficult but if you have any problems you can always talk to me or my sisters."

She drove through the gates and up the long driveway towards the house, both girls stared at each other in wonder. They knew from Emma's accent she was posh, but they had no idea she came from all this grandeur. "I'll show you to your room and let you unpack, and then we will head straight out to the fields. I'm afraid to say, it is Brussels sprout picking, rather ghastly, so wear gloves or your fingers will go numb. She showed them their room and shut the door behind her, as she did this; one of the girls mimicked her accent.

"Rather ghastly." Emma stood back against the wall listening to the offensive mockery taking place in her own house; she had been kind and shown a willingness to be friendly to them. A sudden weariness came over her; everything seemed too much effort. She asked herself what was the point in her doing all of this; no one appreciated how hard she worked. Alone and tearful, she yearned for Edward. Without him, what was the point?

2009

Emma sipped on a large cup of milky coffee and read more about the recession. Things were going from bad to worse, nothing about the year had seemed right, from the beginning there had been a negative atmosphere. Events in the newspapers reflected it and Emma started to panic. She had never been one for superstitions but at that moment she had a premonition. As if by magic Linda May came into the café, she was looking for Miss Attwood.

"I need to speak to you because I don't know who else to turn to." The young girl looked extremely anxious.

"What's wrong, dear?" Emma asked in her usual gentle tone.

"Last night, myself and some friends sneaked out, we didn't get very far because Mrs Granger found us, but on our way back to the school, we saw Matilda and Mrs Granger's husband." Emma held her breath but tried not to show any acknowledgement on her face.

"Why should this be odd?" she asked calmly.

"They were together…" she shifted from side to side, "very close, kissing, that sort of thing." Linda's eyes were wide, searching for Emma's understanding.

"Are you sure you saw correctly?"

"Yes positive and it wasn't just me, Jo, Erica and Louise also saw them. Louise has got such a big mouth. She's telling everyone, soon the whole school will know."

"I better inform Mrs Granger," Emma said with a heavy heart.

"How could Matilda do such a thing?" Linda whispered angrily.

"We don't know the facts yet, try not to judge."

"I saw them together, the facts are there. Mrs Granger has been so good to us, how awful for her. You don't think she could lose her job, do you?"

"I'm not sure how the law works, but I don't think it will come to that. I hope it will just be some misunderstanding."

"What about Matilda? What will happen to her?"

"Like I said, I hope it won't come to that."

"I hope I did the right thing by coming to you. Matilda often talks about you and if I went to a teacher I might get Mrs Granger into trouble. I didn't know what to do."

"You did the right thing, don't you worry I will take care of everything. Don't make any comment to any other pupil and if you see Matilda, please tell her to find me."

"I will."

Betrayal seemed to be a recurring fate in that cottage, she thought. Emma looked around the café; people surrounded with local newspapers and magazines all searching for employment. What a terrible year it had been and for Jill it was about to get a whole lot worse.

Matilda made a quick dash to Emma's bungalow, in a panic she burst through the door. "Linda knows everything! Oh my God, what am I going to do?"

"There's nothing you can do now, just face the consequences of your actions."

"But everyone will be talking about me, I might be expelled."

"Stop thinking about yourself, however bad you are feeling Mrs Granger will be feeling ten times worse."

"I just wanted to be loved; I never wanted to ruin their marriage. If only my parents loved me this would never have happened."

"At what age in your life will you stop blaming your parents and start taking responsibility for your own life? It was you who slept with him, you who lied," Emma put it bluntly.

"Why are you being so horrible? I'm only eighteen and in real trouble and you're shouting at me."

"Yes because you have to learn, that your past and age are just excuses. You know the difference between right and wrong and you decided to take the risk of ruining someone else's life to make yourself feel better. Now you must face up to what you have done."

"And I suppose you have done everything right in your life and never made a mistake."

"I have made mistakes in my life and I'm in no way judging you. I too once had an affair." Matilda's mouth fell open. "He did try to end it but neither of us could, we loved each other too much."

"I don't love Richard," she admitted with a lot of guilt. "I just wanted to be wanted."

"I know you did dear, come here." Matilda fell into the old lady's warm embrace. "I know it looks awful now but somehow, someway things will work out and usually for the best."

"What happened with you and the married man?"

Spring 1943

Edward had watched her all day going about her business, talking to him as if they had never spoken anything but war forms and soldiers. He found her manner unbearable, he didn't know if he wanted to shake her or hold her.

After a long training day, he went back to the large shelter that also doubled up as his office. She sat at his desk and didn't acknowledge his presence as he walked in, not even a smile to greet him. He bent down low over her. "Are you going to continue ignoring me because really, I find it very childish?" Edward whispered angrily in Emma's ear.

"I am being civil and it is not me who is behaving like a child."

"Can you just be a bit friendly towards me, stop being so cold."

"I love you and you tell me not to act cold, what do you want me to do, Edward? Continue as if nothing has ever existed between us. I'm coping the best way I know how and I'm sorry if that offends you but I can't laugh and joke and be friends while all the time my heart is aching." She gave a small sob, his own heart empathised with her pain.

"I hate myself, for putting you through this, I truly do. If I could take the pain away from your heart, I would do, but I am married, I have children." His fingertips touched her chest, feeling her heart beat beneath her shirt and warm skin. Their faces leant towards each other, foreheads touching, "I love you, but I can't offer you anything, if we were found out..."

Emma stopped him by placing a finger to his lips. "Hasn't this war taught you anything, we could be killed tomorrow, people are losing loved ones everyday. We must grab happiness where we can and damn the price."

"Secrets always come out in the end."

"I think we have to take that chance. We may not have tomorrow, but we have today. So let's make the most of it." Emma's eyes pleaded with his, she didn't care anymore, she wanted to be with him.

"We keep this secret for now but sooner or later we will have to tell the world, because life without you is simply unbearable. I love you Emma."

"Show me how much," she whispered in his ear.

Phillip walked slowly over the land of Oakwood, looking out for Maria. When he did see her, she was busy digging in potatoes but still walked over to greet him. "I'm sorry Phillip; you should have given me some warning."

"I know I'm sorry." He had hoped she would come on a walk with him and had stayed out of sight last night so he could surprise her. Now he wished he hadn't. She didn't look particularly happy to see him.

Maria acknowledged how deflated he looked; she felt a twinge of pity for him and decided to change her mind.

"I suppose it is coming up for lunch, maybe we could just go for a little walk." He smiled with an air of relief.

Scarlett had prepared a picnic and left it on a small hill overlooking the farm land. "Potatoes ah, what else gets planted in the spring?" he asked.

"Broad beans, broccoli, brussel sprouts, garlic. But basically everything give or take a month."

"I've started to grow my own vegetables, thanks to you. I think I planted too much though, oh well I will have to send it round the neighbours"

"I bet it will be welcome though."

"Oh yes and now I know what to plant when I go home."

"Doesn't your leg hurt, when you're digging away?"

"Alright you caught me, I don't my gardener does it all."

"Just as well you managed to raise a business, so you could afford a gardener."

"It was my father's business, making toy ships. I expanded the business to making all sorts of toys, dolls and prams. Ships, planes, soldiers and guns, never did I think that actually my factory would be helping to make them for real."

"What do your factories make?"

"Mainly parts for guns but also for planes, because of the war all materials have to go into helping the war effort but we are still manufacturing some toys, just not on the scale it was."

"What is this?" she said as they finally made it up the small hill.

"A picnic, I thought you might be hungry. Would you join me?"

"I would, thank you." It was such a sweet gesture and so surprising, she couldn't bring herself to say no. Phillip lowered himself down slowly on to the rug, which had all been laid out.

"I think I might have to stay here all my life, because I'm never going to be able to get up again," he joked. "I'm afraid it is spam sandwiches."

"It's quite sad how we are all dreaming of a nice white slice," Maria joked looking at the brown grainy bread.

Phillip licked his lips, "Yes, with lashings of butter."

A silence fell between them, Phillip wanted to reassure her, that he just wanted friendship but didn't want to upset her by bringing up the death of her husband. He tried to be as sensitive as possible to clear the air and come to some sort of understanding of each other. "I was very sorry to hear about your loss."

This didn't upset her, she was glad Phillip acknowledged him. Henry was still her husband and still a part of her life.

"I was told, time heals but it's not true you just learn to live with it," she stated.

"When my wife left me, my world crumbled. In a way I wanted to mourn our marriage ending but she had left me and so in another way I wanted to hate her. It was very hard to continue with life without feeling bitter."

"May I ask why she left you?"

"Boredom, I suppose. With my leg the way it was, I couldn't walk, she wanted to be a great actress and dancer. She said I was holding her back. At first I was so angry, I had financed her through her training, for her to turn around and say I'm leaving but now I've learnt just to say thank you. We did have some good times." He shrugged it off as if now he felt indifferent. Maria admired him for not holding a grudge, his ex-wife had clearly used him but he chose to see the good rather than dwell on the bad.

"That is a lovely way of looking at life. Be grateful for what you've got because you never know when it might be gone."

"Many poor souls are learning that hard lesson. Your husband was a very brave man, a hero. Be proud of that."

She smiled and thought of Henry's beaming face trying on his uniform, he was a hero and this kind man who sat beside her said so. She would, forever, be grateful for that.

2009

Jill sat in her office staring at her computer, 'why do machines always break when you need them most?' She wanted to write in her calendar her appointment with the doctor. Instead she wrote it in her yearly diary but without an electrical reminder she hoped that she wouldn't forget or double book herself. Just as she was writing the final word, a knock came at the door. She returned her diary to the top draw of her desk. "Enter." Her husband stood in the doorway, pale looking and shifty.

"Jill I need to speak to you."

"I have some news for you too, but you can go first." So absorbed with his own troubles he ignored the huge hint she had dropped him.

"I have done something stupid, something I will never do again. You have to believe me, it was a mistake. I wasn't thinking straight."

"Richard you are starting to scare me, what have you done?"

"Oh dear God, I can't even bring the words out. I had... I..." he stumbled, with panic.

"Please, what is it?" she was clueless of the bombshell that was about to be dropped on her world.

"I slept with someone else." He waited for a reply but she sat there staring at him.

A hundred questions buzzed in Jill's mind but the shock had left her speechless. "It didn't mean anything, if you ever forgive me, I will spend the rest of my life on my hands and knees, worshipping my wonderful life with you."

Jill gathered her thoughts, she needed information but wasn't quite sure if she could deal with the answers. "Did it just happen once?"

He looked down to the ground, hanging his head in shame. Unable to look at his wife in the eyes anymore he answered. "No."

"It was more than once, with whom?"

"No..." he sobbed pathetically.

"Who is she? A teacher, a friend, someone you met in the supermarket, a man? Who?"

"A pupil."

"No," she said in shock holding a hand to her mouth. "A child?"

"No, she's eighteen and she knew what she was doing, she seduced me. I swear, I never wanted her near me but she wouldn't leave me alone."

"That is no excuse! Who is she?"

"Matilda."

Anger spilled out of her. "You stupid, stupid man! How could you do this to me! Who knows about this?"

"I'm sorry…" he now looked her in the eye pleading remorse, "everyone knows."

Humiliation spread through her. "How does everyone know and I don't? Were you that obvious and I'm the stupid one who didn't see it?"

"We were caught by a group of the girls. Please, I beg you, I am truly sorry. I love you with all my heart."

"Love? Like you know the meaning of it? You are only sorry you got caught. If you had not of been spotted you would of carried on! I just can't believe how you have lied to me. You had promised me love and children and happiness. All the time you were screwing an eighteen year old girl! Have you any idea of the trouble this will cause?"

"What do you want me to say? I made a mistake."

"Get out! Get out! Get out!"

Summer 1943

Emma's life was becoming more hectic, the new girls had no previous training and were often not willing to learn from her. All the girls in the field had a natural respect for Emma since the first day. She simply could not understand why these girls were being so difficult. They heard a posh voice and made an assumption about her. Harvest meant a very busy time. Picking fruit and vegetables and loading up carts, then transporting them all back to the barn, they had to be sorted and stored into different boxes to then be distributed to different places, she did not have time to deal with two difficult girls.

In the glass house they picked the tomatoes taking extra care not to bruise them. "These tomatoes leave an 'orrible black stain on me hands," Jean said as she tried rubbing it off.

"Take an over ripe tomato and rub into your hands that should take it off," Emma told her.

"It works," she said surprised.

"There is no point in cleaning your hands we have to dig up the vegetables now."

"You lot go on," Maria said, "I'll finish up here and then take the cart to the barn. I'll join you later." Leaving the cart to Maria, they made their way to the top of the field. Each girl was given a pitch fork; Tom led a horse over to them with a cart.

"Today's bet is two cart loads," he said to Emma knowing full well she would now do her upmost to beat that."

"Two, more like five."

"Five? Alright, a shilling you won't do five."

"A shilling that I will."

"Deal!"

Emma turned to the girls, who were all wearing their shorts and looked eager to get stuck in. "Right girls we have something to prove, five cart loads and an up your's to Hitler!"

They all cheered and started to dig and cut away the beetroots, courgettes, carrots, cauliflower, garlic, turnips and broccoli. Filling the large carts in no time and happily singing away to 'We'll meet again'.

"If you see any rats kill them straight away. They're Hitler's helpers." One of the girls called to Norma and Joan, both girls made a face at each other. Emma laughed, "We were just like that when we started, now we are completely unfazed by it." Again, they stood there glaring at Emma. "You'll get use to it."

At lunchtime Emma noticed Maria and Phillip going off for a walk. She had taken a liking to Phillip even though it was Scarlett who introduced them; at least it meant Maria was moving on with her life. She continued to work through her lunch, mainly because she wanted the job done but also because she wanted time to think. It made Emma think about the two brothers and how they had both married flamboyant women. Phillip's first wife was an actress and longed for the stage, Scarlett on the other hand didn't quite fit that image. She thought back on how Scarlett had flirted with her brother, it now seemed liked a desperate attempt to get attention but not from William. She questioned why Edward had married her, she found Scarlett shallow and vain but there must have been a time when he loved her. And yet all the time she had known them never did she see him give her any real affection. Why did he torture himself by staying with her?

Her thoughts were interrupted by Tom appearing with a notepad. He had come up to inspect the carts and as Emma had promised, five carts were loaded full of vegetables. Three fields were dug up and fresh manure put into the soil, ready for new seeds. Five horses were tacked to the carts. Two girls to a horse each led them towards the barn. "I'm impressed; you have won your bet. Here you go, one shilling."

Clarice sat at Molly's kitchen table discussing the village and the latest war news. She often liked to go to the kitchen to have a chat but today she had a purpose, she wanted to make up a little food parcel for Scarlett and the children as a special treat.

Emma walked in just as Clarice put the finishing touches to the box. "Dear will you take this to Mrs Grey, just something small for her and her family."

Straight away Emma had a problem with this, "Shouldn't it go to someone who could really need it."

"I want her to have it, she been very good to us and so has her husband. Why if it wasn't for him my Bernadette would probably be dead!"

"They don't need it though or deserve it."

"Emma that is enough, all that sun is making you grouchy. And for your information, Scarlett comes here and knits with me for the war effort and it was her idea to introduce Maria to Phillip, who is a lovely man. I want her to know I appreciate her efforts."

"He is middle class," Emma said, not because she cared but because she knew her mother did.

"We cannot be too picky nowadays and he will look after her. That is all I want for all my girls, someone who will treat you right." She looked at Emma's weary face. "You look very tired and isn't it time you stopped flashing your legs in your skimpy shorts. You will lose your looks with all the stress and work, I really think you should end all this nonsense and start looking for a husband and be quick before they are all killed."

"I made a commitment, I have to continue and as for a husband, I think I might leave marriage, it is too complicated. For me I want total independence, my own money and my own life."

Now Clarice was getting angry at her daughter, "Emma how many times we do not earn money we marry it! Women should not have to concern themselves with money; it is a man's job to keep you."

Clarice often showed little embarrassment in sharing her opinions in front of Molly, who had worked all her life, despite being married to a wonderful man. But today Molly felt irritated by her employer, a rage was burning inside of her and she ached for self-control. She didn't utter a word though for she was just a servant and would have to ignore her employer's disrespectful views if she wanted to stay employed.

"Do you want me to take this box then?" Emma resigned herself.

"Yes go now and invite them all to dinner, make sure you mention Phillip. He must be there."

"I hope you're not pushing Maria, Mother. She is still very vulnerable."

"I know what is best for my daughters and as soon as I have got Maria remarried, I am coming after you." Clarice poked Emma in the stomach tickling her a little bit, which made Emma giggle. "Off you go and remember, invite Phillip."

"These young girls today always have some silly notion in their heads," Clarice flapped.

"Lady Attwood, many people have to work and many people enjoy their work, so if you do not mind I would like to be getting on with mine in peace." Molly's eyes stared at Clarice. Clarice could see them glistening with tears. Normally, if a member of staff had spoken to her like that she would give them their marching orders but Molly had never spoken to her in such a way even when she had been at her most obnoxious and demanding. She had worked for Clarice and the family for thirty-two years, started as a maid at the age of 15 and never had a cross word been said. As insensitive as Clarice often was she knew something was very wrong with Molly today.

"Molly what has happened? This isn't like you." Tears continued to roll down her face.

"My eldest son was killed in action. I found out this morning."

"Oh my dear." In an act of deep rooted sadness Clarice comforted her friend of many years and cried with her.

Emma walked down the familiar path to the cottage, she knew Edward would be at work and Phillip was probably back at home. It would just be her and Scarlett, alone. "Ah, Emma how nice to see you, do come in," Scarlett said as soon as she had opened the door.

Emma made her way through the living room and into the kitchen. "Take a seat, would you like a cup of tea?"

"No thank you." Still holding the box, Emma could not bring herself to give it to Scarlett. Looking round the cottage, she could see Scarlett had everything that she could possible want, nice furniture, plenty of food in the cupboards. Emma noticed a wedding picture on the mantle piece. Edward looked very young and Scarlett very beautiful. A wave of hot resentment came over her as she continued to view the cottage.

Scarlett watched Emma's eyes, viewing her home, a smug glow came over her as she thought, 'see we may not live in a grand house but I can have everything you have got, brat'. Out loud she continued being civil, "What brings you here?" Scarlett didn't want to acknowledge the box, in case Emma handed it to her. The last thing she wanted was charity but if it was from Lady Attwood, she would have no choice but to accept.

Emma sensed Scarlett's unwillingness to accept the box and simply said, "Mother asked me to stop by and ask you all to dinner next week."

"Oh how lovely, do say thank you to your dear mother. We would love to come."

"Great. Friday evening around seven and mother said Phillip is invited too."

"Marvellous. Could you send your two land army girls round later, I'll inspect them for baby sitting."

Emma tried to curtail her anger, "They are not employed to baby sit."

"Oh, they are paid by your father, what we ask them to do, they will just have to get on and do it."

"No, that won't be possible. They are here to work for the war effort and nothing else."

Scarlett normally got a lady in the village to look after the girls but she was hoping to get it for free this time by using the land girls. Despite Emma's protestation, Scarlett would not give up so easily, later she would say thank you to Lady Attwood for the invite and mention the land girls to her. She would get her own way.

"If I do find someone to look after the girls, I'll see you Friday."

"Yes," Emma said distantly still eyeing the photo.

"Is that all?" Scarlett asked rather sharply.

"Yes, I suppose I better go, thank you for your time."

Relieved to be out of Edward's and Scarlett's marital home, Emma made her way into the village of Hawthorne to Mrs Lillie's house. She was a lady of seventy-six years and the oldest person in the village. Behind the overgrown trees and bushes laid a very small beautiful pink thatched cottage. The gate squeaked as Emma opened it and black paint peeled off of it. She knocked on the door and waited a good five minutes before Mrs Lillie opened it. "Miss Attwood, what a pleasant surprise. Come in, come in."

Emma followed the old lady through to the kitchen, watching her hobble from each room. Inside, the house was nothing like the Grey's. The wallpaper was stained and scuffed, the furniture was old but of no value and the whole place smelt of damp.

Worse still the old lady looked ill. "I have brought you this, just a small box of things. There are some vegetables and fruit, butter, milk, small bits of meat and some tea."

"Thank you so much, it is so very kind of you."

"My mother was concerned about you."

"She has already been so kind, I can't thank you enough."

Emma asked if she could use Mrs Lillie's bathroom. "Yes of course, it's outside you can't miss it."

Behind a bush stood a small wooden shed, inside was a toilet. Emma had no idea Mrs Lillie lived like this, no wonder her health was so bad. Then walking back, Emma noticed the roof was looking old and in places she could see the eves of the house. Inside Mrs Lillie gave Emma a cup of tea. "Mrs Lillie, has your roof been leaking?"

"Yes a little but nothing to worry about. I just put a sauce pan underneath it."

"You know we have a field that grows the reed for thatched houses, I could put a new roof on for you."

"OH! No, please don't go to any bother on my account, you have done enough. Plus I couldn't afford it," she admitted shamefaced.

"It's no bother and I'm sure father will agree with me, you can't live like this."

"I feel I would be taking advantage."

"Honestly, I would like to do this. We need the practise anyway."

"Well if you insist." Emma nodded enthusiastically. "You are a good girl."

When Clarice asked her daughter if Scarlett had liked her box, Emma had two choices. Either she told her mother the truth and get into trouble or lie and make Scarlett seem like a saint. "Mrs Grey was very grateful but said she was quite alright for food and tea. She told me to take it to Mrs Lillie instead, but she asked me not to say anything to you because she did not want to offend you."

"Oh, that dear sweet girl, what a kind heart she has. You could learn so much from her Emma. It is just as well you told me or I would be going on and on about it. I won't say a word. Oh I am so glad it went to Mrs Lillie, what a kind heart."

Emma handpicked the girls who would help her on Mrs Lillie's roof; Tom had taken time out to give Emma the basic instruction. "After you have cut the reed you need to put it through a reed comber. You will find this easy, it's just like using the threshing machine. You remember how we did it last year? Put the reed through the machine and out comes the stalk; the ears will come out separately."

The only difference was that Emma could start work straight away she did not need to dry it out first unlike the corn that would be harvested in May and dried throughout the year until November. Putting on some stout leather knee pads and some strong gloves, Emma started to strip Mrs Lillie's roof. The whole thing would have to be complete within the day, so no time could be wasted, despite Mrs Lillie's best efforts to bribe them with lemonade and seed cake. Starting at the lowest point of the roof and working upwards, Emma left an overhang of reed so water would slide off and away from the cottage. Each batch of reed was ten inches across and three inches deep, they had a pull that would bring the batches up to Emma on top of the ladders. While down on the ground the girls would dampen the reed slightly and tie it with twine to make the batches. Three other girls worked on the roof with Emma each at different corners, working inwards. It was a heavy job and despite Emma's protective gear she still got cuts from the reed when she was using the wooden comb to smooth it all down. Each batch of reed had to be tied again and then the twine would be taken over to the next bale and looped around and so on, until the girls met in the middle. From the top of the cottage Emma looked out across the village. Never in her life had she felt so happy, helping Mrs Lillie had reminded her why she had to get up in the morning. She had a reason to fight, along with everyone else; there were people who appreciated her hard work.

When Edward heard about the dinner, he groaned inwardly. He hated these get togethers, especially when he had to listen to his wife and Lady Attwood bitching all night. However, it would be a chance to see Emma, which was so rare. They had both learnt to be cautious but it also meant they didn't get to spend much time with each other.

Scarlett carefully applied her make-up, while watching her husband in the reflection of the mirror. "I think Phillip and Maria will make a wonderful couple. Don't you think darling?"

"I think you should stop interfering. Why do you have to push Phillip, you are only getting his hopes up?"

"He has lost his confidence in himself over the years because of that awful woman. Maria can fix all that and in return he can mend her broken heart."

"You can't just replace people. Love doesn't work like that."

"You have to make the most of life; no one gets what they want so you have to make it work for you."

"Meaning what?"

"Meaning we don't always get what we had hope for. Anyway, with Phillip and Maria together, that means we will see more of the family over the years. Who knows maybe Louise might marry one of the sons, she could be the next Lady Attwood."

"Louise is eleven years old! She is my little girl and you want to parcel her off to the highest bidder."

"I want the best for my daughter! I want her to have the very best in life, to a man who truly deserves her."

"This isn't about what is best for Louise this is about what you want, what you have always wanted, someone rich, so you can look down your nose at other people."

"Do you know what I want Edward? I want a husband who will touch me! I could have married a very rich man, I had someone interested in me, someone who was deserving of me but then I had to go and meet you! You had no problems touching me then!"

"If I wasn't good enough for you then why in the hell did you marry me?"

"Because you got me pregnant or had that slipped your mind?"

"So *you* say!"

"You disgusting pig of a man! I never wanted you! I took pity on a lonely lost solider but when I fell pregnant with *your* child, I had no choice but to marry you." She was panting with anger but would not relive the sad memory of her first pregnancy.

"If you are unhappy, you are free to leave me," Edward said with an eerie calmness. "I will support my children but you can take care of them and when you are ready you can marry some rich fool."

"Divorce?"

"Yes."

"Edward, I do love you. It has taken time but I do love you. This is just stress talking, I understand, we will put it behind us."

Edward didn't have the heart to argue any further, "I'll see if Phillip is ready." As he left the bedroom a knock came at the front door.

Scarlett shouted out, "Answer that, it will be the land girls, I asked them to baby sit."

When evening came the atmosphere in the lounge of Emma's family home seemed tense; an aura of awkwardness surrounded them all. Scarlett was quiet, Edward avoided all eye contact, Phillip nervously rolled his thumbs and Maria tried in vain to think up interesting topics of conversation. Harold stared into his whisky and Clarice complained it was too hot. Emma had been working out in the sun all day and now had a splitting headache, the room was spinning and to compound matters she also felt sick and could not bear the thought of dinner.

"Mother, I am so tired. Would you mind if I go to bed?" Emma said, with total exhaustion. Clarice got up out of her seat and walked out with her daughter.

"You do not look well, should I call the doctor?"

"I just need to lie down." Clarice put her hand to her daughter's forehead. "You're burning up, I should really call for the doctor."

"No please," Emma said earnestly. "A good night's sleep, that's all I need."

"Up you go then."

"Is Emma alright?" Edward asked as Clarice returned.

"I'm afraid she is not feeling too well, she is going to bed."

Edward's heart sank, he wanted to see her. "I really needed to speak to her about some important papers. I misplaced them and I wondered if Emma knew where they were."

"Can't it wait until Tuesday?"

"It wouldn't take me long and they are very important papers."

"Do not worry Major, I will go up and tell Emma you wish to speak to her," Bernadette said.

"Thank you."

166

Emma closed the door slowly, her head was splitting. At first she assumed it was too much sun, but she felt tender as well so then she thought it was her time of the month but viewing her calendar the unimaginable truth dawned on her.

"Emma?" Bernadette came into Emma's room; she lay in bed with her head still throbbing and the nausea rising.

"Yes?"

"The Major wants to see you. Something about missing papers. Should I send him up?"

"Yes alright then."

She dragged herself out of bed and sat by the window. He was quick to see her. "Your mother is not happy I'm up here," he laughed. Emma shrugged her shoulders.

"What papers have gone missing?"

"What? Oh no I just used that as excuse to see you. Won't you come down I need you to cheer me up." He sat down on the floor beside her chair, holding her hand. He was about to tell her, his plans to divorce Scarlett when he noticed Emma's dazed look. "You should be in bed, I'll leave you."

Emma became tearful, feeling so ill and so tired she wanted him near her. "Please don't leave, sit with me for a while."

"You need to rest you're not well."

"I'm pregnant," she sobbed.

Edward was silent, unable to catch his breath. He looked at her, her face full of fear. He pulled her down into his arms and held her tight. "How far gone?" he whispered.

She clung to him. "A few weeks, a month. It could even be two. I can't remember when..." she trailed off, still in shock. "Will you go with me?"

"Go with you where?"

"To get rid of it." Guilt flooded through him.

"You don't have to do that, I will support you." He tried to reassure her but she wasn't listening.

She started to mutter to herself. "I might die. What if I die?"

"You don't have to do that. I will get a divorce from Scarlett." He rocked her gently.

"I'm so sorry Edward." She looked into his pale blue eyes. "I can't do it, I'm too scared."

167

He kissed her forehead, "That's fine. We will tell them together."

"No, not yet please, I couldn't bear it. Mother will throw me out."

"When you are ready, I will take care of you."

Edward was secretly overjoyed; he hadn't planned this but now it meant him and Emma could be together, there was a strong reason to fight. He didn't think about the disgrace Emma was about to cause to her family.

"I better go, remember to take care of yourself darling. If you need me, you know where I am."

2009

Emma knocked on Jill's office door, "May I come in?"

"Yes," Jill groaned. "I suppose you know everything and have come to tell me how sorry you are."

"Pretty much but also to say, and I know you are not going to want to hear this, Matilda is very sorry too."

Jill started to cry, "Everything is ruined, my whole life and she's sorry."

"Have you informed the authorities?" Jill nodded, still choked with tears. "When will you see Matilda?" Emma asked. Jill looked up in shock.

"Why would I want to see her?"

"Trust me it is important to forgive her, not just for her sake but for your own sanity. You need to get her side of the story, until you have that, then you can't make a decision on the future. Also no matter what has taken place you are still her headmistress."

"Do you think I care about her? If I see her I won't be able to control myself."

"Jill, I know you are hurt and angry but you can't blame it all on Matilda. I hate to put this so harshly but she was in your care and your husband abused his position."

"Are you saying I owe her an apology?"

"No but you do owe her a second chance, we all make mistakes. We hope age and wisdom will give us better judgement but we can only learn those lessons by living through them."

"I can't handle this. Why are you sticking up for her?"

"I am not protecting her. I am trying to protect you and all you have worked for."

"Please just go, I will speak to Matilda at some point but now at this moment it is too soon."

Autumn 1943

"Emma, I need your help," Maria said while rushing into her bedroom. Emma lifted her heavy head off the pillow, she had fallen asleep in the afternoon. At three months pregnant a small bump was beginning to show, luckily with the air getting colder, she could wrap herself up in her large oil-skin coat and hide her growing stomach. "Sorry were you asleep?"

"No, no, what can I help you with?"

"I'm going out tonight with Phillip. There is a dance on at the village hall; I have promised him we will only dance the slow ones for his leg." She gave a nervous giggle. "I was wondering if I could borrow a dress and maybe some silk stockings."

"You can borrow a dress," Emma went over to her wardrobe and pulled out a white silk dress. Cut along the shoulders, pulled in at the waist and stopped just bellow the knee.

"Oh that is beautiful!"

"As for the stockings I'm afraid all of mine have been worn out."

"Mine too."

"I have an idea that the girls in the fields do, come on leave your dress here, this may get messy." Emma found Bernadette and asked her to help.

The three of them made there way into the kitchen where Molly was preparing dinner and Doris chatted over a cup of tea and biscuits.

"What are you girls up to?" asked Molly, surprised to see the three of them standing there.

"We need to make up some gravy to paint Maria's legs," Emma explained, as they all fell about laughing.

"Gravy? At least when he says to you, you are good enough to eat, you know he won't be lying!" Molly jested.

At that Maria froze, "It's too soon isn't it, I'm doing the wrong thing." Molly put an arm round her.

"Now love, don't take it to heart, roll up your skirt and let's get painting."

Each leg, ankle and foot was lightly painted with a thin gravy solution. Careful they then drew a line up the back of her leg to make it look like the seam.

"It looks very authentic you would never know," Emma said, proud of her work.

"I smell like a Sunday roast!"

"But your legs look good! Let that dry before you put your dress on."

After half an hour getting ready, Maria looked beautiful. She gazed at herself in the mirror. "I wish I was going out with Henry. I keep thinking that and then I feel really guilty because Phillip is such a lovely man and I do care very deeply about him but…"

"It is just a dance, nothing set in stone. Go and have a wonderful time," Bernadette reassured her sister. "Henry would want you to be happy."

Maria walked to Edward and Scarlett's cottage, Phillip opened the door. "Do you want to come in for a cup of tea first?"

"Yes, that will be lovely."

The house seemed quiet, "Where is everyone?" she enquired.

"Scarlett has gone to her sister's, she has taken the children with her."

"What about Edward?"

"Oh, he's still here working."

"Seems odd, Scarlett going off like that, mother will be upset."

"Well…" he moved slowly towards her, "her sister's husband died last month. Scarlett is comforting her."

"Oh."

"Sorry I didn't mean to bring back bad memories." He noticed Maria's sadness that showed in her eyes.

"Not your fault." She smiled weakly, "Shall we go I'm not bothered about tea now."

"Yes, we can go."

2009

Jill sorted through a short marriage worth of stuff. She cried over photographs, got angry over valentine cards and yearned over the scent in his clothes. She had had enough, the day had been too painful and now with all of Richard's belongings on the living room floor, Jill felt she could not bring herself to be parted from them. Feeling dizzy, she made her way outside to the garden and breathed in the sweet scent of lilac. Small blue forget-me-nots had sprung up everywhere; with everything that had been going on she had not noticed it. Taking a seat, she considered her life without Richard; it didn't seem much of a life at all. Lost in her sorrow, she did not notice Miss Attwood coming up through the house and up the garden path with a small dish of food.

"I brought you over a plate of food; I thought you might not have eaten," Emma said.

"I haven't but I am not hungry. How did you get in?"

"I still have your spare key. I hope you don't mind."

"No."

"I don't mean to be rude but shouldn't you be keeping your strength up?" Jill looked up sharply.

"You know?"

"I guessed it was a possibility. Does Richard know you are pregnant?"

"No and I will not tell him. A relationship without trust is no relationship at all."

"Could you rebuild that trust?"

"We could try, it might work for a little while but I know one day someone else would come along and it might be innocent but the suspicion will be there, paranoia and jealousy. Arguments will start and all the while a child will have to put up with that. My parents always used to argue, they loved each other, just couldn't live with each other. My father died last year and since then, my mother has been devastated. But living in that world, I never knew if everything was going to change in an instant. I never felt safe, Richard gave me that security and now it's all gone. I'm alone."

"You will never be alone."

"I feel broken." She cried heavy tears. "Will the pain of humiliation ever fade? There was a time when society had morals and if something would happen like this then they would condemn them. Now this sort of behaviour is just accepted. A shrug of the shoulders as if to say they are young, they don't mean it."

"But you see, they *don't* mean it that is the whole point. Today's generation is completely different to the one we grew up in. They are exposed to real life from a very early age and all from the comfort of their own homes, TV, internet, magazines and newspapers inform kids of things we would never even think about until we were married. The older teenagers cannot be considered as children anymore and they should not be treated as so, we never were and we didn't know half the stuff they do. And going back to the day when nothing was discussed, didn't solve the problem, it just hid it. How teaching is done today is not enough, a new era of education must take place." Jill wrapped her scarf around her tighter, not because she was cold but it offered her some comfort.

"Isn't it down to parents to inform their little darling of the ways of the world?"

"They don't need to talk to parents anymore, like I said they can get the information they want without any hassle. But what is not explained are the social implications, which if parents cannot talk about then schools should."

"Oh Emma, I thought the same thing once but now I know young people know the system and they know how to abuse it and get away with their actions, and no amount of discussions is going to change that."

"People make mistakes that will always happen, but we live in such an open society and that can only be a good thing. I truly believe we are making a better world and the youth of today will continue that because of the advantages in the changing of people's attitudes." Emma looked at the cottage and wished she had lived her youth today, then at least she would have been allowed to know her daughter and granddaughter. "You know this cottage used to accommodate a family of four, Major and Mrs Grey and their two little girls."

"And?"

"I fell in love with the Major and became pregnant with his child. I couldn't tell my mother she would throw me out and it was too much of a risk to have an abortion."

Jill sat there in stunned silence; this confession came from out the blue. Finally Jill asked, "What happened?"

"Two of the most unlikely people helped me."

Winter 1943

Emma was now six months pregnant, her large bump was covered up thanks to her oil-skin mackintosh and an old corset from the attic. She feared people noticing her weight gain and tried to think of excuses.

The pregnancy had really sapped her energy but she had to seem to continue as normal even though this was difficult. Her back ached, her feet swelled, her temper was short and every problem seemed ten times worse than it was.

Matters were made dangerous one morning when the Friesian bull had escaped from his pen and was in an adjacent field; Emma had never met with such a problem and feeling exhausted she thought it best to ask Tom. "He will know how to move him back to the pen. Go and get him," she asked Maria.

"No, don't bother him," Norma said, "I can move him. What we can do is lay the kitchen food scraps and then let him eat his way back to the pen."

"It means you will have to get close to him. What if he charges?" Maria said, realising the bull would not notice the food unless it was put directly in front of him.

"Trust me I know what I am doing."

"No, I'm going to get Tom." Maria started to walk off but Norma was determined to prove her point. Edging forward she carefully started to throw the food down near the bull, but he took no notice. So she moved closer. The bull on seeing her, grunted, hot air steamed from its nostrils, it misted around them mixing with the cold winter frost. His foot rubbed roughly on the ground, watching her getting closer and closer, invading his territory. In a spilt moment, he charged at Norma, she started to run but he was too quick, his head knocked her to the ground, his horn just missing her skin. Emma grabbed a pitch fork and jabbed at him in the air, threatening to pierce him. For a moment Emma feared he would turn on her but he retreated and she managed to drive the bull to the other yard. Quickly shutting the door, she tried to steady her nerves, her hand shook uncontrollably and her breath was short and sharp.

Norma lay still on the grass, her breathing was deep, the shock and the force of the hit had paralysed her. Emma gave her a hand to get up and slowly the pair walked away. "Thank you," Norma whispered, as Emma held her hand.

"Are you alright?" Emma asked.

"I think so. That thing could have killed me, you were so brave. How can I ever thank you?"

"As long as you're alright and anyway it nearly worked." Emma tried to cheer her up.

"What is all this food doing on the ground?" Tom yelled, hot tempered as usual.

"We thought we would give the bull a picnic," Emma joked, sparing Norma the embarrassment of her mistake.

At lunchtime Emma was still shaking from the morning's happenings when she met Edward. His eyes brightened on seeing her. He embraced her ever growing body but she pushed him away. "We have to tell your parents," he said sensing her upset.

"Oh yes and then, everything will be alright."

"I told you, I plan to take care of you."

"How? You have a family."

"I can divorce Scarlett and I will make sure the children are well looked after."

"I could not bear that."

"What choice do you have?"

"I cannot have your broken marriage on my conscience."

"But you were willing to have an affair!"

"Because I love you!"

"Yes, I love you too. So we will tell your parents, I will tell Scarlett and then we will just have to take it from there."

"No, you don't understand! My background is completely different to yours. It won't just be a few disapproving looks and nasty whispers down the high street. I could be cut off from everything. Family, friends, money, everything, the lot. Can you imagine what would be written about me and my family in the society pages? Lady E. Attwood, daughter of Lord H. Attwood has lured a married man with children and then trapped him by becoming pregnant. Such a scandal could kill my mother."

"You are over reacting. Unmarried girls get pregnant all the time."

"Not in my class!"

"That is what it comes down to! I'm not good enough for the likes of you and your family! I really thought you were different but you're just like your mother a snob!"

"If you hate snobs so much why did you marry one? She is the most obnoxious upstart I have ever met!"

"If you hate my wife so much, why do you care if you should break up my marriage?"

"Because you have children together."

"Rubbish, you just don't want to look bad in front of the posh lot at the manor house."

"It is too much of a sacrifice."

"You lose your inheritance; daddy doesn't buy you new shoes. So what! Walking away from your wife and children is a sacrifice!"

"I didn't ask you to leave!"

"You are such a brat at times!"

"Why don't I just kill myself, that will solve all my problems." With that he glared angrily at her and a cold silence came over them.

"Don't you ever say that, don't even think such a cruel thought. Emma I have told you I will look after you. That's an end to it."

"No, this is the end of it."

"What?"

"I will have to think up an excuse and leave for a bit. I will have this baby in a private place and give it away."

"I don't believe you."

"Believe it, my mind is made up." Cruelly she had taken the decision upon herself without Edward's input into their future.

"Please listen to me, Scarlett and I were never in love. We met one night at a nightclub and she had been her usual flirty self. I was in a bad way that night, I had just returned from the second battle of the Somme and I had done something to save the lives of men and it had got me promoted but if the army knew the truth, I would be hanged for mutiny in the trenches. The Colonel in charge had gone mad; he was stopping the water supply to the trenches. I discussed it with a General who understood the problem but the Colonel was high born. There was no way of removing him diplomatically. So one evening I shot him, there were no questions asked as everyone thought he was mad but the guilt of killing one of our own has never left me. Worst still I was being rewarded for it. I was down and Scarlett was a comfort or a distraction. Whatever she was, she has never been the woman I love."

His confession had not diminished her feelings for him but her mind was unchanged. Emma knew in her heart the reality of confessing the affair would destroy too many people. She loved Edward and life had been so utterly cruel to them but there was no point in deluding themselves they could never be together.

The day had been difficult, shaken by the bull and then her heated argument with Edward had left Emma feeling nervy and distressed. In the afternoon the land girls had to harvest the carrots. Rows and upon rows of green stalks flopped over the mud, planted in between were onions, to deter carrot fly from destroying the crop. Each time Emma bent down to pick up an onion or carrot, sweat formed on her forehead and a shooting pain would travel up her spine, leaving her speechless. Dizzy from the day's action, she fainted in the field. Norma rushed over with Joan close beside her. "Emma is not well, run and get help," Norma said quickly as Emma was coming to.

"No, I'm alright just a bit dizzy." The winter sun burned in her eyes as she tried to look up at a silent Norma and Joan. Both had undone her coat to try and cool her. Now both of them knew her secret.

"We should get you inside."

"Please," Emma's whisper trailed off, feeling faint again.

"Is everything alright?" Maria yelled, who was on the other side of the field.

"Emma's not feeling too good; I'm going to take her back to the house." Norma buttoned up Emma's coat quickly when she saw Maria walking over.

"Oh Emma you do not look very well. Do you want me to help you bring her in?" she asked Norma.

"No, it's alright Joan and I can manage.

Carefully they lifted Emma by the arms and walked her slowly to the house. All the while Emma's mind was whiling. 'What am I going to do? What am I going to do?' her mind would not let that question go. Finally, put to bed she laid there in a haze of thoughts. She kept imaging the baby coming, charging at her like the bull and goring her life into little bits. She could see Norma and Joan whispering behind there hands and laughing at her with the other girls. Edward saying he no longer loved her because she was a brat. She could see her mother throwing her out of the house and her father not defending her and seeing his face full of disappointment. Emma cried out at that point, she could bear anything but her father's disappointment. She was completely isolated; she could not turn to anyone without distressing them all and destroying herself.

When the couple of hours of deep sleep and frightening thoughts were over, Emma opened her eyes and looked around the room. For a moment she tried to remember what was going on in her life and what had happened. With a sudden kick from inside, all was remembered.

Panic filled her, 'what if they all know?' 'Would I still be laying here if they did?' A knock came at the door, dread descended on Emma. "Come in," she said nervously. It was Norma holding a cup.

"Brought you up a sweet tea, thought the sugar might help. Don't tell Molly though, she says we eat more than we get in rations but that is because we burn up so much energy." For a moment Norma forgot why she was there.

"Norma, please I beg you with all my heart, please do not tell mother that I am…" She could not bring herself to even say the word.

"I won't I promise, that's why I've come to see you. Joan and I have agreed to try and help you do your jobs, as well as our own."

"Why would you want to help me?"

"Oi, don't look a gift horse in the mouth. You did save my life this morning. I think that thing would have gored me if you hadn't pricked him with that pitch fork."

"Thank you." Emma wept with relief; her secret was still safe for the time being.

"What are you going to do when the baby is due?"

"I don't know. I'm so scared," she cried

"You know I could ask around, see if a place could be found, you know some where private."

"I know of a place in London. It's getting there which will be so difficult."

"What about the father of the baby, doesn't he want to make an honest woman out of you?"

Emma looked down at her swollen feet, sticking out of the covers. It was bad enough two people knowing she was pregnant without them knowing the father is a married man. "He doesn't want to know." 'Another lie, when did I become this person?' she thought with self-pity. Out loud she continued, "Mother must not know about this or I could be in serious trouble."

"I promise, I will not tell anyone and like I said Joan and I will help with your duties so that should take some of the pressure off."

Emma thanked her once more, she was extremely grateful for her kindness. Tiredness hit her once again; she was mentally and physically exhausted.

A few days later Emma informed Edward she would not be working for him on a Tuesday. Her excuse to her mother and father was that it was getting all too much for her. Edward was not so easy to convince. "I want to stay close to you."

"I'm not going anywhere, the corset isn't really working anymore and I can't wear my coat, while I'm working in an office. The soldiers will see my bump." Edward's hand stroked her stomach.

"I have bought us a house in a nearby village."

"Is that so I can stay there, when I need to get rid of it?" She could not think of that day when she would hold something so precious and then have to hand the baby over to someone else, it all seemed too dreadful for words.

"No, the house is for us. It is near a small hospital, so when you are ready we will tell your parents. I will take you there and then I will tell Scarlett."

"You make it sound so easy."

"It is. Emma I promise to take care of you. Just think of our own little family, waking up with me by your side," he tried to convince her.

"Can you afford it? Remember there is not just me to take care of, there is also Scarlett and the girls."

"Alright so we might have to rough it a bit but at least we will have a roof over our heads and most importantly, we will be together."

"It doesn't change the problem."

"No not here it doesn't but after the baby is born we can move to Devon or Cornwall. We are winning this war now North Africa and Italy are in the Allies hands. It is just a matter of time so maybe after the war we can move to France. No one will know our history and we can start again."

With an excited smile on her lips, Emma began to imagine what life might be like if she agreed to moving. "I will work a few more months. We will need all the money we can get."

"After the New Year, we will tell your parents and leave."

"I'll be eight months then, I bet I will be huge."

"You will be beautiful."

"I can't believe it; soon, we will be a family. What about Scarlett?" Emma said, remembering why she was so reluctant in the first place.

"She is my problem. You just worry about keeping yourself well."

"After the baby is born I can get a night job or something."

"Well that's up to you but you won't have to work if you don't want to. I promise you again and again and again. I will look after you."

"That's the other thing; what about your job? Father won't let you work here."

"I have a few friends in the army, they will find me work."

"What if they send you to war?" she said panicked.

"We will cross that bridge when we come to it. Let's deal with one problem at a time."

Emma wrapped her arms around his neck, "Everything is going to be alright, isn't it?"

"It will be." He kissed her. "It will be."

"It still worries me what people will think of me."

"They will think what I know about you. That you are kind, considerate and warm hearted. Not to mention very beautiful.

Emma knew the truth of the situation as well as Edward, if they confessed he would most likely lose his rank and be sent out to fight, but if it meant they could be together, they were both ready to take the risk.

Christmas 1943

Clarice busied herself with small presents for Molly and Doris, but she could not concentrate. She was missing Scarlett; she had been away now for over a month. Phillip and Maria were getting closer and she had no one to confide her excitement to. When she had asked Edward about her return, apparently she had delayed it until after the New Year. Clarice tutted, 'they could be married by then and Scarlett will miss all the fun.'

2009

Jill sat back enthralled; it was the first time that week she wasn't thinking about herself. "Go on, did you run away with the Major?"

Spring 1944

"Pack your things, tomorrow we will leave."

"I will." Despite the trouble over the last two months hiding her pregnancy, Emma felt it had all been worth it. Edward and she would soon be together.

"Until tomorrow, my love." They kissed and embraced in the knowledge that tomorrow will be the first day of the rest of their lives.

Emma woke up with a buzz of excitement in her belly. She busied herself packing some of her clothes knowing that tonight she would be leaving all this behind. She hid the luggage in the back of her wardrobe, ready to be collected later on that evening. Throwing on her mackintosh, she made her way outside to do the most monotonous jobs, picking brussel sprouts. Bending down repeatedly was hurting her back, but at least she wasn't using any heavy machinery. It also gave her time to think about the day she would hold her little baby and with Edward at her side. She finished her final day and went back into the house to pick up her luggage and take it to Edward's car. They decided that they would be already to go before telling Clarice and Harold. As soon as Emma had walked in the house she felt a cold atmosphere. On hearing Emma, Maria walked to greet her. "Emma, we have heard from Jack?"

"Oh, how is he?"

"He is coming home. He is alive but his plane crashed and sadly he has lost a leg and has severe scarring from the burns."

"Poor Jack, how awful."

"At least he is still alive. Mother is very upset. Father is trying to calm her."

Emma's heart fell, how could she walk away from her family when they were all in so much turmoil? She felt deeply sorry for her brother and wanted to be there for him but it could mean, saying goodbye to her last chance of real happiness but she had no choice, she had to put Jack first. 'He will need me, they all will need me.'

That evening she met Edward at the gate with no luggage, disappointment flooded through him. "You can't change your mind." Edwards's eyes were pleading with her to come away with him.

"Have you told Scarlett?"

"Not yet. I can't put it in a letter; I will tell her face to face. Now please just get in the car. I'll buy you new clothes."

"I can't come with you."

"You're just scared. Please trust me; I will make sure you have everything you need. Ignore what people say, it doesn't matter so long as we are together."

"I can't leave," she cried. "Jack is coming home; he has been badly injured. The whole family is dreadfully upset. I can't add to their problems."

Edward took a deep breath, "If we don't leave now though we might not get another chance."

"We don't know that; just give me a few more weeks."

"You are due in a few more weeks."

"One month, I'm guessing but that is long enough. Please."

"In two weeks we are leaving, no excuses. I will take you to our new house and then I will come back here and break the news so you don't have any stress."

"I know this is a pain but it will be worth it when we are together and I know Jack is alright."

"Take it easy."

"I will, I promise."

"I love you." He kissed her and held her tightly to him. "One day we will look back on all of this and laugh."

"With our seven children," she giggled.

Clarice sat at the breakfast table thinking about her son's homecoming a few days before his arrival. "We should have a party for him," she blurted out

"He has lost one of his legs; I do not think he will be in the mood to celebrate that fact!" Harold retaliated angrily.

"Harold we should show him how proud we are and a party is a good way of doing that."

"I have said no, now that is an end to it."

"What I will do is let him come home and after a few days, throw him a party. That way he has time to settle in."

186

"He will not want the fuss."

"Do you think he has changed?" Clarice asked pondering her son's nature.

"What sort of stupid question is that? Of course he would have changed! He has been to war, bombs, guns, mud, blood, vermin and vomit! Of course he will be different; all he will want is a private homecoming and a bit of peace and quiet." He was regaling his own horrifying experience of war. He had seen men scarred and wounded, shell-shocked and broken. He wondered how his son would cope, if he could cope.

Once again Clarice witnessed her husband's anger; he was always a deep thinker but very rarely had he raised his voice with it. The war had brought back so many deep seated emotions. For a time she could not see the man that she had married.

Jack was helped out of the car and into his wheelchair. "Welcome home son," Harold said holding out his hand, which Jack shook.

"Father," Jack's cold reply came. He wheeled himself to the front steps and groaned inwardly. First humiliation, "Father may I lean on you."

"Yes son." Jack seized his arm and pulled himself up from his chair, when Clarice came running out.

"My dear boy, how good you look!" she lied, throwing her arms around him. His face was dressed in bandages, his leg missing and his body still ached with movement. He wanted to scream.

Harold was desperate to shut her up, "Clarice take the chair indoors."

"What?"

"The chair! The chair!" He used his head to gesticulate where the chair was, while still holding on to his now disabled son.

When the three of them had made it into the living room, Bernadette, Maria and Emma joined them for tea. Emma had watched her brother arrive and came into the house after a few minutes, keeping her coat wrapped around her.

"Take that coat off Emma. How many times I have asked, do not wear it in the house."

"I'm going back outside in a bit."

Conversation stopped for a second, everyone felt awkward looking around the room, desperately thinking of something to say and then saying it three times in theirs heads, making sure it would not offend Jack.

"Now I'm not fighting any more, I wonder what I will do for the rest of my life." He had often dreamed of travelling the world, painting beautiful women in exotic locations. Now he could not see himself getting around much.

"You could become a doctor. Very respectable job is a doctor," Clarice said the first occupation that came to mind.

"I think I have seen enough doctors to last me a lifetime. I certainly do not want to become one."

"No, you're the eldest; you will have this place to run soon enough." Harold thought this might cheer him up, he could not be more wrong.

"Oh yes I could just see myself rolling over the hills," Jack said sarcastically.

"You won't always be in that chair."

"Do you think I will grow another leg then?" Jack didn't mean to shout, his temper kept getting the better of him. "Sorry, I am feeling quite tired, may I go for a lie down?"

"Of course," Clarice said. "Bernadette, help Jack up the stairs."

'Humiliation number two' thought Jack.

Once alone in his room, he lay on his old bed, depression and anger still boiling inside. There was a knock on the door, it was Bernadette again.

"I have brought your chair, in case you need to wheel yourself to the toilet."

'Final humiliation.' He rolled over and shut his eyes; even this gave him no peace. Again he could hear the bullets fly though the air pinging and piecing his plane. The smell of his own flesh cooking still lingered in his nostrils; sweat ran down his face, "When will I be free?" he asked the empty room.

Emma watched her family go through hell, everyday they tried to get Jack out of his room but he wanted to stay there in his dark place with his dark thoughts. She realised there was nothing she could do to help; only he could make the decision to carry on with life. After a week, Emma decided it was time to leave. She met up with Edward to establish the new plan. She told Norma and Joan that she was going to have the baby in private with her mother knowing but did not explain she would not be coming back. For Emma it was hard to say goodbye to these girls, to all of them. Over the past few years friendships were made, a bond like soldiers in the trenches of an unspoken loyalty. To lie to them was the biggest betrayal to her and she despised herself.

"Tonight have everything ready to go but don't bring those cases down with you. They will be too heavy."

"I can't confront mother."

"Keep your mother talking; I'll creep upstairs and grab them. Give me ten minutes then leave."

Emma nodded nervously, "It's going to be sad, walking away from the family."

"Are you sure this is what you want? I would never want you to be unhappy."

"I love you. This is definitely what I want; I just wish… well it doesn't matter now."

"In time they will forgive."

A quick thought Emma said, "Do you think you can get upstairs without mother or Jack hearing you?"

"I am a trained solider, master at being silent."

"That's not how I remember it." She gave him a playful smile.

"What are you implying?" he laughed.

That afternoon Emma said goodbye to her beautiful childhood home, so many happy memories of her brothers and sisters playing together. She knew she had to see Jack even if it was to say goodbye without him knowing. After tonight she might never see them again. Mother, would most likely, cut her off from all the family.

On entering his room the oppressive atmosphere hit her. It was like entering a cave, everywhere was dark, he had pulled all the curtains blocking away all sense of time. He sat on the end of his bed staring ahead of him. His body looked tense and rigid, one wrong word and she knew he would go off like a bomb.

He turned his head slowly towards her, "What do you want?"

"I just wanted to see how you were."

"Fed up, you know now, you can go."

189

"Jack," Emma walked into the room, "you have to stop torturing yourself. I understand that you are depressed but if you don't get up and start moving you will never be able to shake it off."

Jack glared at her. "Why are you here? Just to tell me to go outside, smell the flowers and listen to the birds! Do you know what I have been through?"

"I want to see you happy again."

"I will never be happy ever again!"

Emma had had enough of his self-pity and yelled at him. "Grow up! At least you have come back and will not have to fly again into that hell hole, unlike William and many others."

"Oh yes good old William! He will come back a hero, not a cripple. He had several nurses round him flirting; I'll have several nurses trying to carry me. Being helped by women, it's humiliating." Emma could no longer contain her own anger, she could not see things from Jack's point, she thought only of her own torturous situation.

"Sit there and wallow in your self-pity. It's not the lack of a leg stopping you getting on with your life and making the best of it. It is your own pride that is doing it. You really are pathetic!"

With his good leg he violently kicked his wheelchair into Emma's stomach. He turned away, expecting her to do the same but Emma dropped to the floor clutching her stomach.

"Emma?" He whispered.

He watched as she cried in pain, under her breath he could hear her say, "Don't go. Don't go. We are nearly home."

"Emma? Please what is wrong?" He started to panic. As Emma rolled over to her other side, Jack saw blood on the floor. Nausea rose in him, "Mother! MOTHER!!" he yelled.

Clarice was in her conservatory, watering her plants; she could not hear her son yelling for help.

He knelt next to Emma, she had lost consciousness. He grabbed the wheelchair that lay next to her. He rolled himself to the landing and yelled again, still no reply from his mother.

Gripping the banister, he pulled himself upright and threw his chair down the stairs. Throwing his bad stump over the banister and holding his breath, he slid down, still aching from his injuries. He retrieved the chair and rolled out into the conservatory, which

190

was situated right at the back of the house overlooking the garden. "Mother!" he breathed heavily.

"Oh darling you have come out of that room."

"Mother, it's Emma, she is unwell."

"I know she has not been well for a while and do you think she has gained weight of late?"

Putting two and two together Jack knew what was happening to his sister.

"Mother, Emma is having a baby. Now! Go and help! Quick! Now!"

Clarice froze on the spot, did he say having a baby.

"Mother, Emma needs you, go to her!"

On finally listening to him she ran upstairs and straight away she could hear her daughter's groans coming from Jack's room.

Jack rolled out of the house and down the path hoping to see Maria but it was the Major who was walking towards him. Edward noticed Jack's worried face and quickening his pace forward, his intuition telling him something was wrong.

"Major Grey, please help it's Emma, I think she is having a baby. Please help, she is in a lot of pain."

Running as fast as he could, he ran into the house. "She's upstairs in my room, it is first on the left!" Jack yelled after him.

He saw her lying on the floor with blood running from under the coat. Clarice lay beside her, holding her hand. "I do not know what is wrong with her." Clarice said in a rather bemused way.

The Major picked Emma up and cradled her to him. "Everything is going to be alright, try and stay calm." He gently laid her on her bed and started to strip her of her coat and boots.

"Stop that!" Clarice shouted as the Major continued to undress Emma.

"She needs to get into a nightdress."

"Why? She just had a turn or something; there is no need for all this!" Clarice was still refusing to accept the truth.

"Emma is having a baby! My baby!"

Clarice looked at her daughter then at Edward, the truth hit her cold but it was the shock that made her think fast and take control. Emma's fate was now in her mother's hands.

Clarice walked out the room in a state of shock but a clear idea of what needed to be done, 'Jack was right, Emma is pregnant.' Her mind went to Jack, running downstairs she ran to catch up with him. He must not get a doctor. No one must know of this. Bernadette had heard the noise and had come down to see what was happening. When Jack had told her, she told him to stay put. No one knew Emma was pregnant and she knew her mother would like to keep it that way. Bernadette loved her sister but no way was she about to openly expose her family to gossip and ridicule. Emma had been a silly girl and now she would suffer for it.

"We have to get a doctor," Jack pleaded desperately.

"She's in safe hands, trust me."

Clarice came running through the living room doors. "Have you told anyone?"

"No, only Bernadette."

Clarice slumped down on the sofa, "I want you to tell Molly and Doris to have the day off. I do not care what excuse you give them so long as it is not the truth. Then I want you both to leave the house."

"We should be here for Emma."

"I must deal with Emma alone and I do not think the outcome will be a happy one. It is best you do not witness it."

They both did as they were told.

Clarice paced the floor, thinking over what Major Grey had told her. "She is having a baby. My baby."

'He is a married man,' she reminded herself. 'He is going to walk away and leave Emma with his bastard child.' How could she be so stupid, what will people say? The scandal!

Upstairs Emma tossed and turned in pain, "Emma you have to push," she could hear Edward saying.

"No it's too early."

"We have the head, now push!" Reluctantly Emma pushed hard, she felt the baby's body slide out of her. "It's a girl. We have a girl."

Emma shut her eyes, exhausted and in pain but hearing her baby cry filled her with a sense of achievement. The pain was unbearable and the drowsiness worse. Before falling asleep, she had the image of Edward beaming as he held their baby girl.

2009

"That was the last time I saw my baby and Edward."
"Why? What happened?" Jill asked shocked.

Spring 1944

"You are awake." Clarice sat in the chair next to Emma's bed, stroking her forehead.

"Where is Edward?" Emma asked weakly.

Clarice bowed her head, "I'm so sorry Emma, your baby died. Edward has gone for a walk; I do not think he will be back."

"No…" She whispered in shock. "I heard her cry. Go and get Edward, I need to see him."

"Your baby was premature and weak. Her heart just stopped."

Emma could feel her life being torn apart, only a few hours ago, she could see the two most precious people in her world, now neither of them were there. "I need Edward," she cried.

"I did not want to tell you this, but he blames you. He said he could not bear to look at you."

"No he is not like that."

"You did not see him, he was so angry. I was scared at what he might do to you."

"I love him, I must see him. Let me see him." She tried to move out of bed but the pain shot through her.

"Lie down," her mother ordered. "He told me you did not want the child and that you had done this on purpose, I can understand his hatred of you and I am sure you can as well."

"At first I was scared but I did want my baby, I wanted to be with Edward. You must tell him I wanted our baby."

"He has gone back to his wife. Did you really think he saw you as anything but some cheap foolish tart. I thought you better than that Emma. I am ashamed of you and I dread what your father will make of it all."

"Are you going to tell him?"

"No, if you do as I say this little event will never be known."

She cried with unbearable grief. "What am I to do without him?" She just wanted Edward.

"A few days ago, a letter came for you," her mother continued ignoring her pain. "The land army are very impressed with your work and they want to make you a forewoman. I will reply and say you will do it. It means you working away but at least you will be away from this place."

"Mother…"

"We won't speak of this again. By tomorrow it will be like nothing ever happened."

"Mother was very friendly with Lady Denman, who was head of the land army. I was moved to Kent within the week and put in charge of thirty girls."

"And you never saw Edward again?" asked Jill.

"No, never again and I loved him with such a passion. It still hurts to this day. In 1946 the war was over, the land army but continued for a little while longer; I decided to leave at the start of 1947. I returned home and Edward had gone. All was back to normal, only a few shelters remained. Mother was right, it was never spoken of."

"Was he the love of your life?"

"Yes, he was the love of my life."

"Is that why you never married?"

"After the war, Nickolas came back into my life but so much had changed and friendship was all I could offer him. When my father decided to sell off this place, Nickolas and his mother, who we all called Poppy, asked me to move in with them. Poppy was quite a girl back in her day, my mother was right when she said Nickolas's father was of 'no good stock'. But I liked her, and Nickolas and I got on well, we moved to a three bedroom house in London and I was Poppy's companion."

"Did you and Nickolas ever become more than friends?"

Emma laughed, "Oh yes."

"But you never married him."

"No. You see the time I spent with Poppy was when I learnt about Nickolas. I told you Poppy was quite a girl, a free spirit. She wanted to be a dancer and her father hit the roof. Still he loved her and set her up a bank account. She was living the high life and one night fell for a smooth talker and ended up pregnant. Her father never truly forgave her, arguments were a daily process. Nickolas and his grandmother were always stuck in between the two of them. Over the years though, Nickolas took his grandfather's side, he found his mother's behaviour difficult to accept. So when he asked me to marry him, I could not make that commitment, I never told anyone the truth but I was concerned that he might find out, there was chat in the village and knowing his ethics I did not what to trap him into a marriage that was built on a lie. It would have been a sham and I couldn't tell him the truth, I didn't like the thought of him seeing me in a different light, I suppose I didn't want him seeing me like Poppy. As fun as she was, she had quite a reputation and it embarrassed him. I hated the thought of embarrassing him, of him being ashamed of me. So I risked him walking away from me rather than tell him the truth."

"But surely he was upset that you never agreed to be his wife and living with you! Didn't that hurt his ethics?"

"Yes, but after the war, when you have confronted death so many times, a bit of love is better than nothing. Anyway he thought I was doing it to annoy my mother, maybe I was."

"What about children?"

"I never fell pregnant again. I think I would have married him if I was having his baby but it wasn't meant to be." Jill held her stomach, thinking on her own situation. "Last year I received a letter from Edward's solicitor. He had died years before and left me this letter but they had only just found me." Emma held out a crumpled piece of paper. "I keep it always. It is his writing."

Spring 1944

"You have a healthy beautiful baby granddaughter," Edward beamed at Clarice.

"I don't want to look at it. We put trust in you to look after her and you took advantage!"

"I love her with all my heart, we both wanted this, so please just be happy for us. I have bought a house, Emma and I plan to be together."

"You really are deluded! I am not going to let a common soldier waltz off with my daughter! One who has shown himself so clearly to be beneath all decent society."

"If that is how you feel then fine, but Emma and I will be together. You can't stop her."

"I am her mother, of course, I can stop her! She will have wealthy men throw themselves at her. Whisk her away to their castles and keep her in the style she has become accustomed to. Do you think she will give up a chance like that to live with you?"

"You don't know your daughter at all! She isn't like you and your stupid ideas about how people should dress and talk, she couldn't care less. She takes pride in her work, she likes helping people. You don't deserve a daughter like Emma! She loves me, why can't you just let her be happy!"

Scarlett now walked into the living room. She had just got back and had come round for her cup of tea and a bit of a gossip with Clarice, but as she reached the living room door, she overheard everything. Now she confronted her husband. "You have been having an affair with that obnoxious girl!"

He was shocked to see his wife but Edward wanted to fight for Emma. He no longer cared who would get hurt, he wanted to be with the woman he loved. "Emma is kind, loyal and selfless; I love her because she is everything you're not."

Scarlett slapped him hard across the face, expecting a heated reaction but to her horror he just turned his head. Watching him for a second she begged, "What about our children?"

"I don't know if they are mine. Do you?" Again he threw his doubts in her face, humiliating her in front of Clarice, it was cruel so she chose to be crueller.

Scarlett smiled callously at him before turning to Clarice. "I will take the child."

Clarice's face relaxed in relief, "Will you do that?"

"Yes bring it down; I will register the birth straight away."

Clarice ran upstairs, leaving Edward in absolute disbelief. "You can't do that! I won't let you; everyone knows you have not been pregnant."

"No one knew about Emma, I will just say I hid it so not to make a fuss and gave birth at my sister's."

As soon as Clarice walked in with the child, Edward cuddled her to him. Clarice now spoke to him. "Do you really want Emma to live with the stigma of bringing up an illegitimate child? Because if she leaves here with you, I will not have her back. You are getting older, you will lose your job here and be sent off to war, you will most likely be killed in action and leave Emma alone to bring up a child in a village that will despise her. Is that what you want for her?"

He held the child close to him, trying to think. Scarlett carefully took the child from his arms, "This is for the best." She started to walk away before turning back to Edward. "And if you ever think of leaving me, I will treat this child like the bastard it is."

Hot tears came down Edward's cheeks. He felt ashamed to be so overcome by raw emotion, but the thought of never seeing Emma again broke his spirit. "It is for the best, if you truly love Emma, you would want the best for her." Clarice started to push him forward.

Slowly he walked away knowing he had lost for now, but he had their child, he would always do his best for her because he could not do it for her mother.

"After that is was bitter, mother had controlled my life. She had no consideration how I felt only what other people thought."

"Things could have been so different for you."

"Yes, they could have been, but I don't think I could have been much happier. Nickolas is a wonderful man and I do love him very much, but it is a different kind of love, not like I was with Edward and I think that is why I am so happy. I see Nickolas for who he is, not what I want him to be."

"What about the rest of your family?"

"Jack became an artist and never had to use a wheelchair again. William came home with the French nurse he had married. That got up mother's nose! Maria married Phillip in the end and moved to Cornwall. I grew close to my niece, Elizabeth; she would stay with me and Nickolas during school terms. Not being able to have children meant Elizabeth was the next best thing. I was staying with her when I turned up here. After father's death, mother went a bit funny in the head; I suppose you could say she always was," Emma laughed. "Bernadette and her husband sold off the rest of the land. The money was spilt."

"So you are still living with Nickolas?"

"Yes, he is visiting a relative. A cousin, who lives in Scotland but is from the Doverenski family. They have only just learnt of each others' existence. I told him to go as time is short and I had Elizabeth to help me move in."

"Does Elizabeth know about what happened?"

"Oh, yes, she was there when I received the letter. I was in a terrible state and I blurted out my life history to her. When I showed her the letter, she saw Edward had written my daughter's full name at the bottom of the page. Elizabeth looked it up on the internet; her name came up straight away, how she had married the president of a car manufacturer. A story about her walking out on her husband appeared, saying after the death of her mother, she had some sort of breakdown and had left her husband and daughter."

"Do you know where she is now?"

"No, but I know where my granddaughter is."

"Matilda?"

"Yes, imagine my surprise when I found out she was here."

"Have you told her?"

"No, I wanted to see her but I knew I had no claim over her and I never intended to get embroiled in her predicament."

"I'm sorry, I still can't forgive her."

"She is just like me, fancying unavailable men."

"I suppose she has done me a favour. Richard never really loved me, I don't think. When I first got this job, the head of education threw me a party; he said to Richard that he was lucky to have such a clever wife. His reply was, 'I don't know about that but she irons a bloody good shirt!' Pig."

"You might still work it out."

"We need to talk that is for sure."

"Some things are worth fighting for even if they are flawed."

The night ended in quiet reflection, Jill made up the spare bed in the guest room, she didn't want to be alone. It would be the first time Emma stayed in Edward's cottage.

Jill sat in her office; she had just received a phone call from the head of education. It was decided Jill would not be losing her job because Matilda's father had spoken to Matilda and she had taken all the blame. Richard would be investigated but that would have nothing to do with Jill. "Could he go to jail?" she had asked in shock.

"It is most likely, it is very serious."

As Jill hung up the phone, Matilda had walked into her office. "I told my father it was my entire fault. I am really sorry."

"I know you are. You know it will go to court."

"I have been told this."

"For the rest of the year you must keep your head down and work, understand?" Jill gave Matilda a weary smile.

"Yes... I am really very sorry."

Jill nodded, too exhausted to be angry and too relieved not to be losing her job.

Nickolas entered into the hallway with his fishing kit blocking off doors and scraping Emma's new flooring. "Nickolas is that you?" Emma asked.

"Yes darling, I'm back."

He walked through to the conservatory, "This is a nice place, I'm glad we decided to move back. Oh I'm sorry I didn't know you had company."

"This is Matilda, we have become friends over these past few weeks. Why don't you go and put your things away and have a shower."

"Yes I will do that." He nodded at Matilda; her face seemed so familiar like Emma's mother almost.

"I better go and leave you two alone," Matilda said.

"Not yet. I have something to tell you…" As Emma breathed in deeply to get some courage, she looked down at Matilda's homework diary, sitting on the table, on the front cover a photograph was stuck to it. It was of a family, "Is this your mother?" Emma pointed out a woman who looked exactly like she looked when she was nearing her fifties.

"Yes, how did you know that?" Matilda said baffled.

"You look like her and who is that?"

"That's my grandmother Scarlett Grey. She was wonderful, always full of life and fun. Good for a giggle and those two are my aunts and the two boys are my cousins. We were such a happy family. After grandma died, mum was devastated. I'm still in touch with all my other family; I much prefer my mother's side. My father's side of the family are awful, there's only father's sister and she doesn't have any children, so I like having a big family on one side. Sorry what did you want to tell me?"

Emma stared at her granddaughter. "I have enjoyed getting to know you Matilda and I feel that there is some sort of bond between us."

"Yes I feel like that too, you are my fairy godmother."

"I'm afraid I will not always be around to protect you, but if you ever find yourself in a sticky situation then sell this." She pulled out a Fabergé brooch. "It belonged to Nikolas's mother and she gave it to me. It is very expensive so you must take care of it, promise me."

"Miss Attwood, I can't take this."

"I have no children to pass it on to and I want you to have it to remember me by. Please look after it."

"I will, I won't ever sell it and I won't ever forget your kindness towards me."

"Now you listen to me, you do not need the validation of men to prove you are worthy of love. You do not need to behave impurely or dress in a provocative manner. Men can be very immature, there is no need to demean yourself to that level. Always remember you are worth more than that and you deserve to be treated with respect, but this is down to you seeing yourself in this light, not men. If you think you are worthless you will be treated like that and you are not, you are smart, kind, funny and beautiful. You have got it all so make sure you only settle on the best."

"Like your Nickolas."

"Yes, exactly right."

"I will repeat your words to myself everyday, thank you."

Emma saw Matilda to the door. 'It was for the best,' she told herself. All her life she had hated Scarlett, but clearly she had brought up her daughter with all the love and care as if she was her own. Why spoil that happy image in Matilda's head for her own happiness. She had been a part of Matilda's life even if it was just for a little time and had given her some guidance.

Nickolas reappeared with a small crystal fish. "For you," he chuckled. "Has your friend gone?"

"I will not be seeing her again," her eyes lowered as the blurred vision of Matilda walking down the road, disappeared from her sight.

"Emma," he said gently. "I know the truth and seeing the young girl and the family resemblance confirms to me you know the truth as well."

The clock ticked as his words unscrambled in her head. "How do you know?"

"A few days before your mother died, I went to the hospital to sit with her. A woman turned up and all of a sudden Clarice got very agitated, she started rambling incoherent sporadic words. The nurse had to sedate her, but I gathered something had taken place something that upset both of them deeply. Scarlett introduced herself and I took her for a coffee, she was very distressed. I admit I tricked her into believing I was William but the story was a puzzle and I knew she would fill in the missing information if she thought I was one of the family. I was informed about the relationship and the child you had with her husband." Emma sobbed with defeat but Nickolas continued to comfort her.

"Emma, the cruelty of their actions never left their conscience, but as she unburdened herself I could see in her eyes she had guilt but no regret. I told her to contact you, I even told her when you would be alone but she withdrew. Later she confided she had lost her first child. Perhaps your child filled that less. she wasn't there to change the past just to make sure the truth was never exposed to you. Please understand I wanted to tell you, but as far as I was aware you thought you had lost your little girl, and your mother had lied, she was dying, couldn't steal the last good thoughts you had of her."

"I would not have known then. I only found out a few months ago. How different things could have been if I was told then," she sighed regretfully.

"I knew she wasn't going to let you be a part of her daughter's life because that is how she saw her, she was her daughter now. I didn't want you to go through the pain. I did the wrong thing didn't I?"

"This isn't your fault, not any of it, if only I had trusted your good nature and told you everything about my time during the war. But I was frightened of you leaving me again; you don't know how it hurt me the first time." His tired old hands took Emma's.

"Is this affair the reason you never married me?"

"I always feared you finding out the truth and when that fear dissipated over the years, it was too late. I couldn't have you questioning my change of mind."

"Will you marry me now?"

Tears rolled down her cheeks, "Yes."

204